"The Happiness Triangle"

(The Equilibrist series: Vol. 1)

Erasmus Cromwell-Smith

ERASMUS CROMWELL-SMITH

The Equilibrist
® Erasmus Cromwell-Smith II.
® Erasmus Press.

This is a work of fiction. Names, characters, businesses, places, events, and incidents are either the products of the author's imagination or used in a fictitious manner. Any resemblance to actual persons, living or dead, or actual events is purely coincidental.

ISBN: 979-8-9866136-7-3
Library of Congress Number: 1-5005768371
Publisher: Erasmus Press.
Editor: Elisa Arraiz Lucca.
Cover and Interior Design: Alfredo Sainz Blanco.
Proofreading: María Elena Peña, D. Suster, Tracy-Ann Wynter, and Chloe Manuel.
Second edition.
Printed in USA.

erasmuscromwellsmith.com

Erasmus Cromwell-Smith Books

In English

(Inspirational/Philosophical)
The Equilibrist series:
• The Equilibrist (Vol. 1)
• Geniality (Vol. 2)
• The Magic in Life (Vol. 3)
• Poetry in Equilibrium (Vol. 4)

(Young Adults)
The Orloj Series:
• The Orloj of Prague (Vol. 1)
• The Orloj of Venice (Vol. 2)
• The Orloj of Paris (Vol. 3)
• The Orloj of Munich (Vol. 4)
• Poetry in Balance (Vol. 5)

(Educational)
The South Beach Conversational Method:
• Spanish
• German
• French
• Italian
• Portuguese

(Sci-fi)
The Nicolas Tosh Series:
• Algorithm-323 (Vol. 1)
• Tosh (Vol. 2)

As Nelson Hamel*
(Action-Thrillers)
The Paradise Island Series:
• Miami Beach, Dangerous Lifestyles (Vol. 1)

(Sci-fi)
The Rebel Hacker Series:
The Rebel Hackers of Point of Point Breeze (Vol. 1)

* In collaboration with Charles Sibley.

En Español

(Inspiracional/Filosófica)
La serie el equilibrista:
• El Equilibrista (Vol. 1)
• Genialidad (Vol. 2)
• La magia de la vida (Vol. 3)
• Poesía en equilibrio (Vol. 4)

(Jóvenes Adultos)
La serie el orloj:
• El Orloj de Praga (Vol. 1)
• El Orloj de Venecia (Vol. 2)
• El Orloj de Paris (Vol. 3)
• El Orloj de Munich (Vol. 4)
• Poesía en Balance (Vol. 5)

(Educacional)
El método conversacional South Beach:
• Inglés
• Alemán
• Francés
• Italiano
• Portugués

For my children:
"Our blue unicorns in life only exist if we can see them."

Table of Contents

Note by the author,

My name is Erasmus Cromwell-Smith II. I am a scholar and a writer. This book is the story of my father. It is the account of his 2017 poetry class at a New England College. Throughout the years of my tenure, I received several requests from his former students asking me to tell the story of that particular class. I must confess that it took several requests until I became curious enough to spare the time to read about the anecdotical experiences his students had that year. They were right; the more I read, the more intrigued I became until finally I decided to do it to honor his legacy. However, from the beginning, it was a complicated task, as shortly after his passing, his precious archives were sadly lost in a fire, and even though my father wrote extensively throughout his life, for a reason I still do not wholly understand, he never made public any of his poetry. Thus, his literary legacy is limited to several works of fiction published over the years, which did not help me with the task at hand. In the end, the best sources of information were the students themselves, as most still had vivid memories and even some of the class notes. Both allowed me to recreate all the subjects covered that year and more than enough of my father's own words. But the most difficult of all tasks was to find the books, scribbles, scripts, manuscripts, and writings he used for that class. In the end, it took several trips to his hometown to unearth each one. Fortunately, I was able to retrieve them all, including precise narrations of my father's mentoring sessions found in copious and detailed diaries left by each of his three mentors. As you will see, it was a worthy effort that once completed allowed me to bring out his world of poetry for you all to enjoy forever. It is with great pride that I introduce to you my father, Erasmus Cromwell-Smith.

The Equilibrist

The old brownstone building complex has housed the Royal Cambridge Scholastic Institute for more than two hundred years. The top-ranked New England educational institution has a rather British flavor quite fitting to its rich traditions, rigorous discipline, and demanding curriculum.

However, no one embodies better the character of the prestigious school than Professor Erasmus Cromwell-Smith. His thunderous voice is paused in cadence, quasi-perfect in diction, and as hard and heavy as it gets in a Southern English accent.

Everything about the never-married and childless sixty-two-year-old professor is worn and wrinkled, including his tweed jacket with leather shoulder pads, cashmere cardigan, leather briefcase, face, hair, shoes, and even his glasses.

And yet, as unkempt and mundane as he appears, his students describe him as an "awesome teacher!" or, borrowing from a great American, an "insanely great" poet. But the taciturn and circumspect pedagogue simply transforms himself when he commences each of his poetry classes as if morphing from a seemingly catatonic state into a stampede of charisma, knowledge, light, and endless patience.

What nobody knows but his doctor and himself, is that earlier in the week he had been diagnosed with a very aggressive and incurable form of brain cancer that, barring any miracles, will soon incapacitate him from doing what he loves most in life.

Not prone to inaction, and much less feeling sorry for himself, Professor Cromwell-Smith quickly makes a couple of significant resolutions. First, he will treat each day as if it is his last; second, he will reveal in his class a series of life-long secrets he has treasured over the last fifty-four years.

So, in a way, his class of 2017 is fortunate. They will be the recipients of an unknown but valuable gift from the great old master professor, albeit at the risk of being interrupted at any time, perhaps permanently, by his terminal illness.

A young woman with long golden curls is the first to arrive. She has been looking forward to taking his class ever since she heard Professor Cromwell-Smith recite a poem from the Chilean Nobel Laureate, Pablo Neruda.

Today, the students sense something new as the professor walks in at a faster pace than usual. There is tension in his jaw and by the way he is pacing with quick strides back and forth, something he never does, it quickly becomes obvious that he is eager to start, irrespective of whether every attendee is ready.

He then interrupts the classroom's nagging buzz with his opening words for the new year.

Chapter 1

Freedom and Equilibrium

"In my class, the most important rule is punctuality, just be on time for everything. If the class is at eight, show up a few minutes early so you can be ready and fully prepared by eight.

"This year our class will be a journey into the world of poetry, but with a twist, as through narration and reading, I will be taking you to the place where I was born and grew up," the professor says, pulling out a stack of crumpled papers from his well-worn leather briefcase.

"Here we go."

I was born in 1954 in the small town of Hay-on-Wye in Wales. Back then, my birthplace was still medieval, and I mean it literally, not only in its ways and architecture, but also due to the mentality of much of the population.

There were many traditions, and all of them were so rigid as to defend the village's own character and folklore, shielding it against the winds of change blowing across the entire kingdom.

My unintended birth occurred while my parents were still living in post-war Britain that, almost a decade after the end of World War II, still had open wounds, painful scars, and continued to suffer economically, especially in the countryside where some reconstruction and repair of civil works were still taking place.

Entire families had been decimated. It was common that at least one of their members had not made it back from war. Others had come home severely wounded physically, many others, emotionally. Britain at the time seemed split into two worlds. A significant portion of the country had moved on, but the rest was still getting over the devastating armed conflict.

My hometown however, with its hamlets and cottages, pubs and narrow streets, and hand-painted store signs (always in picturesque but opaque tones), has something unique about it. The whole town has countless "antique book" merchants. Each small shop holds aged books of immense value and importance, a few being the only surviving copy. Others are exquisitely written, painted by hand. Each store has its own share of mysteries and secrets. Many of these books are amazing labyrinths of knowledge ready to be explored. Some of the stores are quite sizeable in a cavernous type of fashion. Ancient books surround you, some in piles, some in wooden cabinets, they are everywhere you look. Some books are off limits, others preserved in air-ventilated locked containers. Inside the town's army of bookshops, on one side the scent of old paper and leather combines with plenty of dust, then, on the other are the erudite, in some cases eccentric and mysterious store masters, that often are, the owners themselves.

Thanks to my insatiable curiosity and willingness to become acquainted with these knowledgeable shopkeepers, I was raised between these bookshelves.

Throughout my younger years, I met often with the brightest and most tolerant of this unique breed of antiquarians, those willing to put up with an annoying and quizzical youngster returning, again and again, to learn from them and their treasures.

I left town for good in my mid-teens, thanks to a scholarship to Oxford. By this point, I had delved into countless mysteries and wisdom that I have never shared before with anyone. But all of this happens a lot later...

It starts right after my eighth birthday. I first see him at Mrs. Coe's shop. He has this incredibly funny-looking handlebar moustache that curls on the sides and he keeps on rolling. He has huge and inquisitive green eyes, and his lips are all bundled up into the shape of a tiny frozen kiss. Curious, I peak from afar at all his movements, until he pays and waves goodbye, tipping his tam-o'-shanter to Mrs. Coe. As he leaves, he glances over and squints at me. Then, for no reason I can discern, I follow him staying twenty steps behind, until eight streets later when he steps into a bookshop and just a couple of minutes afterwards, I do as well.

Little do I know that by doing so I have stepped into a world that is going to steer my life into an endless journey of discovery and quest for knowledge.

"Come right in, come on young lad, don't be shy... You must be into books, right?" says the man I've followed.

"Right, sir."

"Well, well, well. You've come to the right place," he says flashing an enormous smile while still twirling his eccentric moustache.

From then on, once a week after school, I would roam for hours through what became my favorite place on earth, 'The Morris-Rose and Sons' antique bookshop (est. 1832). This I do, until Justin Morris IV, the shop owner, not only gives me a space to sit and read, and for us to chat, but also chooses for me a leather-bound manuscript that quickly seizes of my attention, and over time becomes a door into a world of wisdom and wonder.

Yesterday as I saw him busy with customers, I tried to enter quietly, but my clumsiness prevailed. First, the door's old bicycle bell, wound and unwound in slow motion, then I tripped twice over the same old book. So much for my entrance.

Today, as I walk on pins and needles through the store to my tiny reading place, my heart quickly picks up pace when I see from afar the gold burnished pages of my gigantic 'good old' book waiting for me. Sometime later, after all his customers leave, he comes by and sits with me.

It has now been a timeless two hours with my eccentric, self-appointed mentor, a fortunate and quite fitting circumstance indeed, for a single child with a very active imagination, a natural gravitation toward the land of dreams and a keen propensity to the world of books.

"Why are the pages and the letters so large?" I ask.

"There are some who claim that those were the only sizes of paper available then. There are others that assert that in the absence of proper lighting and proper reading glasses, writers needed to

magnify everything they wrote in order to see well enough what they were doing."

"Freedom lies within you?" I read and translate the Old English aloud, dictionary on hand, my tone asking for validation. However, it is pointless, as I cannot understand a word. After countless days trying to figure out the giant, old book, I remain stuck.

"In life, there are always alternating forces pulling and throwing us into extremes, a flow that gravitates like a pendulum from one extreme to another."

"Balance is to be free within life's pendulum, as if within the swings of a metronome."

I sit totally still and gaze in frustration at the hand-painted image on the oversized yellowish page. He stares at me with benign eyes and the endless patience of a genuine pedagogue.

"Erasmus, lift the book and look at the spine from the top," he requests.

I see a piece of paper wedged between the leather cover and the spine. I clip it with my fingers and open it.

"Go ahead, read it."

"The Quibbler and the Street Juggler"

*Standing by the corner
under the broken streetlamp,
on a dusky, foggy and misty night,
the quibbler does what he always does,
he mumbles and grumbles, rambles and tumbles,*

his thoughts and words about anyone and anything.

His big blue eyes dart in near darkness,
right and left, left and right.
And they seem, while filled with magnetic intensity,
as if about to pop out,
of his eye sockets!

And as he stares,
trying to follow the pirouettes of the lonely shadow,
he wonders aloud,

"What is it with this fellow?"

Down the street, unaware of being watched,
he juggles while sitting high above the cobblestones,
pedalling the single wheel in quick bursts,
while glued to the saddle,
contorting into impossible angles
and acrobatic circles,
always defying gravity.
Backwards, downwards, upwards, and sideways.

"He juggles while in balance,
his hands are always keeping multiple objects
floating in the air,

but never handling more than two at once,
despite the swings, twists, and turns,
he never loses focus nor concentration
and does it all with absolute confidence and resolute
determination.

"Yeah, yeah, yeah, but why juggle?"
the quibbler rambles non-stop.
"And so what?
Who cares about living a life on the edge
filled with contortions and near misses in every other corner?

"Because that's what we do in life.
We juggle and seek to maintain balance,
and through practice and experience
we want to master both, as he does,
as if they were second nature to us."

Finally,
reason prevails and the quibbler concludes,

"As the juggler,
again and again,
we strive and we struggle through the streets of life,
sometimes by defying the impossible
and the improbable.

That's what we do,

we seek, we find, and we conquer,

then hang on for dear life.

"To maintain balance and be a master juggler,

requires a disciplined and constant effort,

as they are both a couple of the keys,

to a wholesome and well-grounded life."

As I finish reading, I visualize the movements of the acrobat; I can feel and almost touch his freedom.

"So, in life, you must juggle to be in balance, but to be able to do so, you will need to learn and practice endlessly as both will give you the knowledge, experience, and self-confidence to execute impossible things fearlessly. Mind you, that as with the quibbler, you'll always be surrounded by ignorance and pessimism. The naysayers will always be out there until your results overwhelm them. Above all, never forget that to maintain balance takes continuous hard work," says my mentor.

I do not want him to stop, but that's him. Accurate, in motion, brief, and to the point.

"All right then," Mr. Morris says emphatically, already busy choosing our next reading.

He flicks through the book's huge pages until he finds it, then sets the book wide open right in front of me. I see a hand-painted image of a tightrope walker high above the patrons, on the right side, and

I see the poem for the first time. I glance through it and then start reading it aloud.

"The Equilibrist"

*Our lives are like those
of circus equilibrists.
We walk through a thin and narrow,
but very strong wire,
our emotional life.
The wire is our support system,
made of thousands of filaments
tightly wound together.
Along it lies, among others,
our feelings, our faith, our friends, and family.*

*Equilibrium is tough and challenging,
as it requires endless focus, rehearsal, and attention,
just as the wire does,
life swings,
up and down and right and left.*

*As the tightrope walker
slides each slipper forward,
as if caressing the wire,
his feat as our lives,
becomes a balancing act.*

The more he, like us, practices equilibrium,
the more knowledge and experience he acquires,
the more self-confident he becomes,
because a man on a wire
requires near perfection
for each of his well-choreographed moves.
Without a solid emotional life supporting us,
like the wire of an equilibrist,
there is no balance in life.

When we fall into excesses of effort (like work),
or excesses of freedom (like fun),
we lose equilibrium
and fall from the wire.

And the safety nets down under,
if we have them,
become our lifesavers.

When supported by the wire,
and if we attain sound self-confidence,
we can walk unaided
through the swings of life.
But the ultimate balance
is only attained by the equilibrist,
with the stick,
which is <u>love.</u>

"Are we all equilibrists, Mr. Morris?" I ask.

"No, but we all should seek to be one," he replies.

"Besides not falling from the tightrope into excesses, why?"

"Balance is one of the foundations of happiness. But as important as balance is, the true message lying underneath this writing is about inner freedom. As you can see, freedom is perilous and since it only begins within you. Its exercise requires a kind of self-confidence that only experience and knowledge can provide.

"My boy, there's no truer expression of the power that inner freedom gives than the performance of an acrobat. He not only thrives on it but performs because he calls on it for strength."

I gradually realize that I am the one who has to be free inside.

"Freedom lies within me," I blurt out, nodding and quietly smiling with tight lips.

The words linger, caught in the old bookshop's stuffed air and over the rows of antique books that today have fulfilled their mission in spades with me.

And that's how it all starts, with four words. Me, a young boy fascinated by ancient books, and a wise old man who becomes a guiding light, a life mentor whom from then onwards and forever I've called, The Equilibrist.

Time has evaporated in a blink. The dismissal bell snaps the class and the professor from the trance they are in, back to the present.

"Class, next week we'll continue with my life's journey."

Chapter 2

The Land of Dreams

Today the young woman with long curled golden hair sits in the front row, eagerly awaiting his arrival.

Professor Cromwell-Smith has never seen such behavior. It is 7:50am, ten minutes ahead of schedule and his students are all seated, quiet, and ready to start. He knows that he has captured not only their full attention but also their imagination. He stands up with a broad and quizzical smile, and then out slips the word that has become one of his monikers.

"Awesome! Good morning, everyone."

"Good morning, Professor Cromwell-Smith," they reply in unison.

"Let's go on then. This time I'll introduce you to someone who's been very important to me since my childhood."

Paris-educated, the kind and ebullient middle-aged lady received the finest education at La Sorbonne. Shortly before the commencement of World War II, she fell in love with a French circus acrobat. To the great disappointment of her parents, theirs was love at first sight. Thus, as soon as she graduated, they married, and from then on, she followed him wherever the circus went. But their idyllic life and extended honeymoon were interrupted when he was called to serve his country. Sadly, not long after his departure,

he was killed in action. His trip of no return left her a war widow, all alone at their "circus off-season" tiny residence, in a small village near Cannes, in the south of France.

Eventually, she made her way back home to Wales and upon arrival, took the helm of one of her family's businesses, the generations old antique children's bookstore. This suited her fine, as she harboured a love for reading. Even though over time there were numerous suitors, she never opened her heart again. Her only love in life was her books. This was of course, until I showed up.

Everything about Mrs. Victoria Sutton-Raleigh is small. Her voice, her hands, her feet, her store, but mainly her books, which are really, really small. I visit her every Tuesday and she treats me to tea with milk and Scottish shortbread biscuits. The tiny 'Sutton-Raleigh Book Store for the Young' (est. 1893) is known throughout Great Britain and beyond as the best there is in antique children's books. 'Mrs. V.', as I call her, feels like a grandmother to me and she loves to read to me. At her shop, I am in my element, feel like my age, and there is nothing hard to understand or follow.

"Young Erasmus, what about dreams today?" she asks.

"Dreamy lad. That's what Mrs. Coe calls me every day," I reply.

"Well, that's a compliment, young fellow."

"That's not how it sounds, Mrs. V. I believe she means it to mock me," I protest.

"No matter what others think, to dream is to contemplate life through magical magnifying glasses. Dreamers are like wizards, Erasmus. Would you like to become one?" Mrs. V. asks.

29

"Oh yes, I would."

"Hop in then, let's go for a ride."

Mrs. V. then sits in her burgundy Chesterfield chair, and I squeeze in by her side and simply let her take me along into the world of dreams.

"The Balloon Salesman"

The young man with the tam-o'-shanter
wanders around the park,
a cloud of balloons follows him wherever he goes,
and one by one the small children
come and go away,
with their balloons softly tied to their little fingers.

"Balloons, balloons for sale.
I sell them for a bargain.
I've got Reds, Blues, and Yellows.
Round, Tear Drop or Heart-Shaped.
Just pick one and this may be your LUCKY DAY!"

The whisper of a voice comes from nowhere,
The balloon salesman turns
to face his small customer.
He is flustered, as his sudden move

tangles the lines and balloons above him.

The child stares at the salesman, arms crossed, slightly tilted head
and the pose of a quite amused
but still potentially good client.
"How can I help you, sir?"
"Why, do you sell balloons?"

As he untangles himself,
he gazes benignly at his inquisitor.

"That's a very good question, young man.
Actually, what I sell are dreams."
"Dreams?"
"Well, as people grow old,
they either lose the ability
or desire to dream,
so, it's easy to buy one from me."

"But I do not see any adults buying balloons."
"That's right, only children like you
seem to have an interest, let alone pay,
to walk away with their dreams,
tied in a knot around the fingers,
floating above their heads wherever they go."

"Why do we dream?"
"To chase our truest wishes and desires."

He arranges his balloons
into a tight formation above him
and is finally able to face
his diminutive interrogator,
who has not moved from his wide stance
even one inch.
"But very few kids ask
as many questions as you do.
So, tell you what kid:
today is your LUCKY DAY!
Your curiosity is about to open new doors for you.
I will take you for a ride
into the world of dreams and of imagination."

Then a giant balloon, with the colors of a rainbow,
softly lifts them up into the open skies
and drifts slowly towards the endless horizon.

"When we dream, we float above reality.

"From a balloon, the fields look greener,
the trees seem lusher,
the buildings and the streets

appear neatly organized,
and the lakes and the rivers seem like
the blood vessels of nature,
because as we hover,
everything moves slowly underneath,
allowing us to see and appreciate better
the details in life.
As in a dream,
there's no direction in a balloon flight,
hence we journey without a destination
and that in turn provides us with absolute freedom,
that's because we have no constrains
and feel unfiltered,
when we dream we see the truth about ourselves,
and visualize, wish and think about life and people,
the way we really feel about them.

"When we float from above, we are also able to see
The magnificence of life,
The perfection of nature and
The harmony and sheer magnitude of the universe."

Slowly, the giant balloon descends back to reality.
Then, the balloon salesman ties a big one
with bright and shiny colors
to the child's middle finger,

and he walks away happy
with his dream floating above him.

"Balloons, balloons for sale.
I sell them cheap!
I've got Reds, Blues, and Yellows
Just pick one and this may be your LUCKY DAY!"

I keep rocking my head, smiling with my lips closely sealed in a clownish fashion, as I feel that my dreams are actually floating above my head, and are only being held from flying away by tiny strings wrapped around my fingers.

"Mrs. V., I live in a balloon all the time." I admit, slightly puzzled.

"My dear, what a wonderful gift you have," she chuckles.

"But why does the world of dreams belong only to the children?"

"That's the challenge for every adult, isn't it?"

"Do people simply stop dreaming as they grow old?" I ask.

"Yes, they do, as they let reality control their ability to feel and wish without filters."

"I guess a life without dreams is a life without color," I say, rather gingerly.

"It's a dull and sour life and it is one lived stuck on ground level," Mrs. V. nods.

"Does dreaming make you happy?"

"Of course, it does, since inspiration and blissfulness are required in order to dream, and both are a couple of the most essential ingredients of happiness."

"Then, Mrs. V., when I dream my mind's not in charge?"

"Spot on, my apprentice. When you dream, your brain is nothing but a silent witness, an archive of your life's files from which your dream factory pulls out all the content material it needs for your dreaming activities."

Mrs. V. stands up, walks down the aisle, and picks another book on a shelf right behind her desk. She smiles at me as she walks back with her reading glasses on the tip of her nose. They seem as if about to drop, while she looks down for the right page. As she approaches, the scent of old leather and ancient paper, the antique wall clock ticking, and my sorceress mentor all feel rather magical to me.

"This is a wonderful piece about a young boy just like you."

"The Boy in the Picture"

The boy leans forward with his hands on the soil,
his legs bent, his feet off the ground
except for his tippy toes.
He is ready to bolt like a sprinter.

But his head tells a different story.
With his neck overextended,
tilted to one side,

he gazes in the distance.
Is it an intense stare?
Is he just observing attentively?
No. His body implies nerves.
His body denotes tension
while his head exudes calmness,
one body, two tales.

He is actually peeking, that's what he is doing.
He does not want to be seen,
as he is watching something he is not supposed to.
Something he has been told countless times not to.
And yet, he still goes and does it anyhow.

So, what is he doing...?
He dreams.
He dreams despite the intense lights
coming out of the barn in the distance.

His neighbor, a funny-looking and -sounding hermit,
builds homemade rockets and sends them high
up into the sky.

The boy dreams about the magician farmer
that makes the impossible real.
He wonders at his stubbornness

and sheer determination,
despite his rockets failing again and again.

The boy marvels at his creativity
and unlimited energy.
'That's what I want to be,' he reasons.
'I want to reach the stars, the planets
I want to fly into space and the universe.'

'Through him, I've learned
that anything is possible,
even though at home I am told it's not,
even if I am forbidden to watch,
even if those close to me
don't know what it is to dream.'

The boy leans forward even more.
He visualizes the life ahead of him.
He is already living in the future.
He knows what he wants.
He knows where he is going.

And his journey begins right there,
kneeling on a dirt field,
while peeking at a forbidden rocket factory
in a barn

of an unlikely farmer-rocketeer.
It begins with an improbable
and seemingly impossible dream
from a boy in a picture.

"That is you, isn't it?" she asks.

"Yes Mrs. V., that's definitely me."

"Erasmus, always remember this, nothing can stop you from dreaming. When you dream you visualize how you want to shape your future and when you dream there is no limit to what you can achieve."

The sound of the bell again snaps them out of the time machine and judging by the looks on the students' faces, it is not a very well-liked sound indeed.

"Class dismissed," says the eminent professor as he stands distractedly juggling with memories of his past life.

Too much of a coincidence? the young woman with the curly blond hair asks herself as she leaves the classroom, perplexed.

Chapter 3

The Power of Resilience

As the wise professor rides his old bicycle through the autumn leaves he wonders, given his condition, how much longer, even how safe, it is for him to do this balancing act every day.

I suppose you'll only stop after you hurt yourself, he reflects, predictably concluding the only way he is capable.

No way, that'll only ground me while I heal. Resilience! That'll be today's subject, the absent-minded professor reasons as he steps into his class. Then, as he faces his students, he seems flustered as he vividly remembers the moment in time he first learned about it.

"Class, today I will cover a period in my life when I learned about willingness, determination, and how to never, ever give up, so let me take you back in time, just a couple of years later in the story."

Shortly after my 10th birthday, I, albeit reluctantly, start to play rugby every day at school, but I have a serious problem: I keep twisting my ankle every time I step onto an uneven surface. It is not only painful, as each time my ankle becomes swollen as if stung by a bee, but it is also discouraging, as it sets me back in my training with the team. Finally, I am fitted with an orthopedic inner sole for my right foot and like magic, the problem is gone! Nevertheless, my ankle still gives me the perfect excuse for my parents to end my short foray into the world of sports. Long live the world of books!

Justin Morris IV, the Equilibrist, was born into wealth, vast wealth, going back three generations. Unfortunately, almost all of it was wasted away by the poor judgment and drinking habits of his father, Justin Morris III. What was left of it still provided him with three wonderful deeds. First, a life experience of having lived all over the world with his family. Young Morris IV first lived royally for several years in India. That was followed in equal fashion by Melbourne, Cape Town, and, finally, Shanghai. Second, he received a superb education at Eton, and thirdly, the family-owned antique bookshop in Wales was left to him before the debacle took place. Justin quickly fell in love with the shop, as his passion for books also became his calling in life. His handlebar moustache turned into his trademark as an eccentric antiquarian. Divorced for many years and his children already grown up, my admission into his life has been driven at least in part by paternal instincts soaked with his longing for the gone-by childhood years of his kids.

'I feel like an understudy, so what? Nothing wrong with being a replacement,' I tell myself.

Today, Morris-Rose and Sons has been quite busy with visitors from London. Mr. M., as I sometimes call him, has displayed endless patience with his customers, ending in me helping him cart away twenty books up to their vehicle.

"There you have it. One month's worth of sales in just two hours," he says, grinning.

'He's happy,' I realize as I restrain from showing my darker side, which wants so badly to complain about having to wait those very same two hours.

"Mr. Morris, it's been ten days and the ankle has not buckled again, I do not know how I managed to continue practicing and playing, but I did," I say, conveniently omitting my definitive desertion from the world of exertion.

The store is rather quiet in the absence of customers, but my senses are all in a heightened state of receptivity. I can hear the little sounds of the world of books, a page being opened or closed, a book being pulled or filed, a drawer moving, doors squeaking, all in an endless cacophony in the background of my thoughts and readings. The Equilibrist is busy canvassing an entire shelf, until high up the wooden ladder he pulls out a thin blue book. The silhouette of the old man standing at the top of the step. Rays of light seemingly filtering throughout his body. He is waving enthusiastically at me with an old book in his hands. It is an unforgettable moment, as it is both a delicate balancing act and an awesome display of sheer passion for what he loves to do the most.

"Dear boy," he says, "Resilience is a virtue that will carry you through any hardship or obstacle, and if you make it part of your core, weaving it into your essence and your nature, it'll never leave you. Here's something to that effect, why don't you read it for both of us?"

"The Gift of Life"

When you hear the whispers of sorrow,
counter them with dreams of tomorrow.
When you feel the trappings of failure,
fight them with the thrills
and excitement of being alive.
When you feel emptiness and solitude,
counter them with your faith and heart.
When you find yourself in the jaws of defeat,
push back with conviction and grit.
When you feel zapped and exhausted,
tumble it by recharging, recovering with zeal.
When you feel consumed by poisonous anger,
dissipate it with grace and forgiveness.
When you feel trapped and without options
in life's endless labyrinths,
conquer it by turning around and around,
looking and searching, but never, ever, giving up,
until you find the way.
And when you have defied life in such ways,
always remember that such feats,
are always
what is expected of you,
what is required of you,
wince you were given the 'gift of life' by God.

"So, every challenge, grievance or pain, every obstacle or mountain to climb has a counteraction to overcome them. Thus, you never sit still waiting for things to happen. You should never fail to react even if your reaction is very little or no action, and always remember that in the overall scheme of things, you are accountable and you must be grateful for your life," advises the Equilibrist, *"But what drives resilience is our own inner fire. When we learn to recognize and harness this, it gives us indomitable strength."*

Mr. Morris quickly flicks through the book until he runs into a page filled with reds, yellows, and blues then starts to narrate with passionate cadence and a voice filled with emotion.

"The Unwavering, Unflickering, Tiny Little Flame"

At the very deep end of my heart,
in a place where emotions are raw,
where feelings are unedited,
at Love's nest and launching pad,
and where passions reign free,
with indomitable force,
lies this unwavering, unflickering,
tiny, little flame
that simply
won't go away,

won't quit, won't die.
It just continues to burn and churn,
steadily and stubbornly,
with overwhelming heat and
unstoppable intensity,
no matter what, no matter when.

Its serene hues of blue and yellow
are stunningly beautiful,
its blinding reds and oranges
are breath-taking and powerful.

Thus, I ask myself,
'What is life without our tiny little flame?
What are we without it?'
Well, we either live a life
in black and white or one in full technicolor,
with our inner fire endlessly burning within.

At the very deep ends of my heart,
filled with feelings, emotions, passions, and love
lies this unwavering, unflickering
tiny, little flame
that simply,
won't go away,
no matter what, no matter when,

44

it simply won't quit,
it simply won't die,
it never wavers,
it never flickers,
it never ends.

This is the first time that I see Mr. Morris overcome with emotion.
Now, I value myself a bit more as I realize and understand that there
are strengths within me that I just need to learn how to recognize,
tap into, and use to succeed in life.

"That'll be all for today. Next session will be… let's just call it, magical, and leave it at that," says Professor Cromwell-Smith, wrapping up.

This time the class does not leave after the professor is gone. He later learns that they stayed and quickly formed a social media team to create a forum and a discussion group about his poetry class.

Millennials effortlessly disrupt anything classic or traditional, he reflects in amusement.

Chapter 4

The Magic in Life

Today is Tuesday and Professor Cromwell-Smith is running late. He has been searching for hours for his favorite children's book and when he finds it, there are only ten minutes left to get to his classroom on time. He is not going to make it by bike. Through the window, he sees a campus patrol car going by. He bolts out of the house and starts to run behind it.

"Stop, stop!" he yells.

"How can I help you, Professor?" asks the officer through the window.

"I need a ride. Without you driving me, young man, I won't make it on time."

"Hop right in Prof, this is not an unusual occurrence on campus for you absent-minded geniuses."

"Uhm," says Cromwell-Smith in a distracted fashion.

The guard simply nods his head in resignation, as if accepting that some things never change. In the end, the professor steps into the classroom with a couple of minutes to spare.

"Class, today I've brought with me a copy of a book that made such an impression on me when I was a child that I kept going back asking Mrs. V. to read it to me one last time. The book is called *The Magic in Life* and is simply loaded with it. Let me take you there."

My parents and ten of my friends have just celebrated my 11th birthday at the theme park in Blackpool. I must confess that my interest in wizards, sorcerers, and magic in general, has been sparked by a couple of books that I read at Mrs. V.'s store. Unfortunately, the magic shop that just opened on Main Street deflated most of my fantasies, as I learned all the stupid tricks behind the illusions, so, as it happens with Christmas, there is no magic and there is no Santa!

It is Tuesday afternoon and Mrs. V. realizes I am in a bad mood from the moment I step into the store.

"Calamitous, calamitous calamity!" she utters, and her magic quickly seizes me. "There is no room for grumpy spirits in this shop."

"There is no magic, Mrs. V., it is all a farce. It does not exist," I sigh defeatedly.

"Wait a minute, disappointed sorcerer, what are you talking about? There is magic everywhere, in you and all around us. Have a seat and I will run a literary incantation on you. I will read to you something absolutely magical."

Mrs. V. then pulls out a book filled with blue and yellow colors; it has a little bronze metal lock consisting of two small swinging doors with a tiny keyhole in the middle of the book. Mrs. V. pulls out of her coin pouch the smallest key I've ever seen and opens it. Then she sits next to me on her Chesterfield, finds the text she wants and starts to read it to me with profound joy in her voice.

"The Magic in Life"

What is it?
Is it just light that filters and flows
through everything,
or colors and tones that paint it all?
Or the forces of nature, sometimes sleeping giants,
some others, roaring thunder?

And where is it?
Is it in the overwhelming scenery
of the high mountains?
In the translucent green of the tropical seas?
Or in the serene beauty of flowers?

Is it on the sun exploding in thousands of reds
as it sets in the horizon?
Or on the moon shining through the night sky
in endless shades of white?
Is it just to gaze at the innocent smile of a child,
or the little dog wagging his tail,
or the loving eyes of a mother?
Or is it the countless stories
of Grandma's wisdom?
Or is it about the family sitting at the table,
laughing, arguing, and sharing after a meal?

Or is it just being here...?

And where does it lie?
Is it only in the simple things,
or does it lie in kindness?
Does it lie in passion, happiness, or equilibrium?

Is it in the exhilarating high of winning?
Or in the deflating low of losing?
Is it in the passionate enjoyment
of competitive sports?
Or in the quiet solitude
of extraordinary individual efforts?

Is it in the majestic flight of an eagle,
or the indestructible frame of an elephant,
or the outer space sounds of a whale,
or the deadly jaws of a croc?

Is it in the endless beauty of a piece of art,
or in the dazzling fantasy of a great movie?
Is it in the guilty pleasure of a magnificent meal,
or in the feast to the senses of a timeless tune?

Is it within the silence and peace
of contemplation and meditation,
or in the never-ending enrichment
of spirit and soul, through faith?
Or is it in our ability to distort mundane reality?

Is it in the world of <u>dreams, fantasies,
and imagination?</u>
of those who dare and risk to?
or in the world of creators, inventors, and tinkerers
that turns <u>them</u> into art, products, and crafts?

How about in the contagious ingenuity
of endless hope?
Or in the disarming innocence
of unstoppable enthusiasm?
or passing moments of true genuine happiness
when the trumpets of Heaven play
our 'Echoes of Life',
or is it in the atonement of our faults and errors
through the power of forgiveness and humility?

Or is it simply in the smile of he who wakes up
every day, happy and thankful to be alive?

Or is it in the all-embracing clash

between endless passion and flesh?
Or is it simply when you are truly in love
and your heart does not belong to you?

Where is it then,
this enchanted life God has given us?

What is it,
this magic spell that gives us
the privilege of being alive?

The answer is in all the above,
and much, much more.

Because there is never-ending and endless joy
every second we are alive!
The answer lies within us, and it is self-evident,

The Magic in life is everywhere!
And in everything around us!

And in order to capture it
You only have to LOVE LIFE!
as it has been given to you.

"Young Erasmus, there is magic after all, isn't there?" the old woman enquires.

"Mrs. V., you are a true wizard, and your books are your magic wand," I reply, in awe.

"If that is so, then would you be my young sorcerer apprentice?"

"I already am! So, that's it, Mrs. V.? All I've got to do is love life?"

"I would add, son, love yourself, love others, and love life, and all of it will be magical, or rather, a magical miracle for you."

"I was wondering, Mrs. V., what do you mean for me? And what do you represent in life for me?"

"We all need those special people who bring out the best in us," she smiled.

"So, what are you? My mentor, my guide, a self-appointed granny?"

"Here is what I am to you..."

She opens the book right in the middle and a mythical figure's beauty jumps right of out the pages at me, especially its color, and then she starts to read.

"The Blue Unicorn"

Wizard, Wizard!
Bring me a blue unicorn,
one that sprinkles magic into life,
innocence and candor to the spirit,
light and color to the soul,

passion and love into one's heart,
meaning and purpose for each and every day
that we are alive.

And in a snap!... I am staring at my dream.
In awe and wonder, I contemplate my fantasy...

Let a spell be cast, Wizard!
Let me have a unicorn,
let it be blue as the clearest
of all skies,
and let it be strong
as to conjure all the forces of the universe.

On my unicorn, I want to ride through life,
on an endless journey,
around and around,
and make of the ups and downs,
a "merry-go-round" of effortless
and well-lived circles.

Wizard, wizard
bring me a blue unicorn,
one of those that makes life
a magic carpet ride,
one that makes it all worthwhile.

If there are moments in the life of a child when their entire being denotes total happiness, this is definitely one of those. I hug Mrs. V. whilst dreaming a thousand different things that I could do with my blue unicorn and for the rest of my life have kept it alive as one of those fantasies that never leave you, replaying in your head in countless variations, over and over again. In a way, ever since, my blue unicorn never ever left me.

"We all need one in life, Erasmus."

"I don't need one, I've already got one."

She smiles at me and caresses my forehead while running her fingers through my hair.

"Young man, you are fortunate then, as our blue unicorns in life only exist if we can see them."

Today the class has run over by thirty minutes. No one has noticed the bell. Professor Cromwell-Smith has been finished for almost a minute as his students come out of a quasi-state of hypnosis one by one. Then, something unexpected happens. A couple of students start, and then the entire class stands up and to applaud the professor.

Chapter 5

Courage

Professor Cromwell-Smith is standing next to his old bike with a flat tire. He is constantly checking his watch and seems flustered. An older man also riding a bike approaches. He stops, pulls out a little can from his seat pocket, and hands it to the professor, giving him instructions on what to do with it. Professor Cromwell-Smith hesitates, looking clumsy as he works on his tire. The old man, seemingly frustrated as well, drops his bike, pulls the professor away and applies the can to the tire nozzle. With the tire promptly repaired, soon they both are on their way riding their bikes once again.

"Professor Lichstein, today you are my savior," says Professor Cromwell-Smith, trying unconvincingly to be friendly as they pedal along.

"Cromwell, you better learn some of the basic things in life. Like the kind you need to survive. The mundane stuff."

Both teachers steadily approach the faculty building, then they park next to each other and walk towards the building.

Professor Cromwell-Smith walks the hallways more absent-mindedly than usual. By the time he enters his classroom however, he is totally focused on the task at hand.

He is on a roll. This morning he had to ask several students to leave, as they did not belong in his class, but rather were planning to attend it while standing in the aisles. He left them with the promise that he would do his utmost to get an auditorium available next week.

"Let's move right along then. Today, I'll introduce you to my hero, an exceptional man that has had a great deal of influence on my life."

Nigel Newton-Paine is a war hero. At the end of World War II, he was one of the few British officers flying American planes. In one memorable mission, he saved the lives of his entire crew. He brought home his flying fortress bomber with only one out of four engines working, a piece of its right wing missing, and the fuselage riddled with bullets. The gunner and his co-pilot were severely injured, and parts of the landing gear were broken. Then, once on the ground, Newton-Paine passed out the moment he turned the remaining engine off. When he was finally removed from the cockpit it was discovered that he had been shot in the abdomen and pelvis. The injuries were so severe that it took him months to recover; he never flew again and was left with a significant limp due to the crippling hip damage he suffered from the high velocity gunfire he sustained during the air battle.

Newton-Paine Arts Books and Collectables (est. 1949) is among the newest of all antique bookshops in Hay-on-Wye. After a short stint in Her Majesty's intelligence service, Nigel decided to become an independent entrepreneur doing what he loves to do, which is to read and read and read about art and music. I visit Mr. N. every other week on Fridays, as I have never been totally comfortable with his ways and personality. He is too eccentric and aloof to feel entirely at ease in his presence. His cane too, hanging on the wall, inspires fear in me. I don't know why, except that my instinct is to keep my distance. And that's how when I see him it is an exercise of contemplation on a one-way street; bottom line, I am not a participant, but just an observer. But it is all worthwhile, as everything I learn from him makes me grow, widening my horizons and seeing beyond what I normally see. Today, I am sitting by myself and feeling deeply sad. My auntie, Catherine Cromwell, passed away earlier this morning after a long illness.

"Young man, I've heard the news and have a couple of things that may help you, but first, let me ask the following questions: Can we see beauty when in pain? Can we still hear the music in spite of tragedy? Can we contemplate adversity with respect, but without fear? Can we be right in the middle of a storm and truly believe it will pass?"

He picks up a big volume then, placing it on his lecturing podium, starts reading to me.

"A Song in the Rain"

Today I woke up
staring at a choice,
feeling inspired,
I recall how difficult

it has been

to arrive at such a crossroads.

Is happiness a choice?
I've asked myself
again and again,
again, and again.
In the end, the answer lies
in the most unexpected
of places,
a song in the rain.

The music notes feel wet,
awash by the downpour.

And yet,
the music quietly irrupts
and pushes its way through.
The song comes through the rain,
the tune and the melody deafen
the sound of the raindrops.
I can hear the music everywhere,
as the sky drums like a waterfall.

And yet,
Nothing! can stop the beauty
and the power
of a song in the rain.

"But how can there be music in the rain?" I ask.

"If you can hear and feel music spreading in spite of the rain, then not only can you overcome anything in life, but you can also enjoy it even in the direst of circumstances."

"A song through the rain, I like it very much, Mr. N., thank you," I say, pondering the thought.

Then as I am about to leave, he speaks again.

"Stay a bit longer if you care to do so, I've got a little something here that'll make your auntie both timeless and unforgettable, here it goes..."

"Way, Way up There"

Way, way up there
where one can almost touch the sky,
well beyond the horizon,
there is an endless rainbow,
filled with extraordinary colors,
so bright and so shiny,
that they are a feast to the eye
beyond wonder.

And it points to the sky,
and through it,
after being picked up by an angel,

engulfed in magic stardust,
soared at lightning speed,
your loving aunt,
as she leaves earth,
on her final journey.

And way, way, up there,
where one can almost touch the stars,
forever Catherine sits,
after a journey,
she could not quite finish.

Way, way, up there,
where infinity lies,
just look at the night sky,
and gaze at the shining star,
see how it glows,
watch how it sparkles.

That's your auntie, your mate,
That's your new journey companion,
now illuminating your road ahead,
as you complete your own journey,
through planet earth.
Way, way, up there
where one is in heaven,

where glittering rainbows end,

sits a new star,

that watches your back,

and is your guardian forever.

Overcome by emotion, I walk through Mr. N.'s store absorbing the beautiful words as their calming effect take hold of me. As I wander, I notice the awards on the wall and start to read each one, not realizing that I am stepping into another rabbit hole.

'Ace pilot saves the lives of his crewmembers' reads the framed article encased in mahogany and glass. A medal hangs next to it. I turn around and there he is, the man with a pronounced swing of the hips moves around the store, instinctively fixing, aligning, and putting back in place book after book. I cannot take my eyes off the brave man; he reminds me of my auntie. She was as gregarious as him, a natural-born busy bee, but the similarity that has put me in a trance is far more emotional. She suffered from a degenerative hip, and her body movements as she toiled were almost exactly the same as my librarian mentor.

"How does it feel to be a hero?" I ask hesitantly.

He is already walking toward me with yet another frame. This one contains just a piece of wrinkled, yellowed hand-written paper. As I look at it, the scribble is almost impossible to discern.

"Dear boy, old fighters don't open up easily. We simply hurt too much when we unearth deep buried memories. And yet, mentoring

you makes it almost effortless, as there is nothing more disarming than the innocent eyes of a child or a young man like you.

"Let me show you. See the stains on the paper? That is blood from an airman on his deathbed when we were both convalescing at the airbase hospital. He heard about what I'd done and asked to see me. A couple of nurses wheeled me over and he gave me this. To this day, I don't know if he wrote it, but I do remember vividly the only words he uttered: 'Courage trumps any army and obliterates any fear.' Hours later he passed away."

"Can't read it, Mr. N."

He smiles.

"Let me oblige. I'll do my best not to get too emotional."

He clears his throat and begins.

"A Strong Group of Few"

Once upon a time
there was this strong group of few.
They came from faraway lands,
they had wills of steel,
their flag was engraved on their hearts,
their country was sculpted on their spirits
and their loved ones carved on their souls.

And their courage trumped any army,
obliterated any fear
and their overwhelming and indomitable fury

neither could be contained,
much less halted.

And when the time came to defend and conquer,
their brave hearts roared, and the earth trembled,
and they fought for one another with honor,
to defend and protect their flag, country,
and loved ones.

Then the devastating force of their valor
crushed it all,
leaving nothing in its wake.
Once upon a time
there was this strong group of few.
they came from faraway lands,
they had brave hearts
and they could not be conquered
as
their flag was engraved on their hearts,
their country was sculpted on their spirits,
and their loved ones carved on their souls.

At night as I walk back home, I can feel the violent vibration of the
flight control handles and listen to the roar of the remaining single
engine as Mr. N. brought his plane back to his home base.

This time, Professor Cromwell-Smith is the one who comes back from the past to an entire class that is just staring at him; they don't want it to end.

"That'll be all for today," he says as he stares at nothing, still firmly stuck in a world of heroes and incredibly brave men.

Chapter 6

Anger and Life's Circles

Sometimes he can't help it. Professor Cromwell-Smith is not a morning person. Feeling a bit old, and anxious about his deteriorating health, on this particular morning, he is grumpy. When feeling this way, he always tries to remember what he learned from Mrs. V. long ago.

Shortly thereafter, having adjusted; emanating passionate enthusiasm, a resolute professor walks in ready to share one of his favorite secrets.

"Class, sometimes our days do not start well, and yet, it is still our burden and challenge, as it is entirely up to us to steer them in the right direction. I still remember vividly a very particular day when I was handed a valuable life lesson."

"Mrs. V.!" the cabbie yelled at the poor old man crossing the street. The milkman was shouting at a couple of kids who accidentally broke a few of his precious bottles as they crashed their bikes into each other. Then, the mailman shouted at a pregnant lady because she did not come out fast enough to collect her letters. The bartender cursed while throwing the drunk man out of the pub. The Indian man at the newsstand damned our creator as a teenager spilled a soda on his magazines. The plumber called upon his co-worker's mother when he accidentally broke a pipe they were

working on, and the policeman vented in frustration chasing a youngster for loitering in the wrong place. My history teacher pleaded for heavenly assistance to grace me with wisdom and responsibility, and my mom chased me out of the house when I told her that she had a new brand white hair above her right ear lobe.

"Has everyone gone mad? What is going on?"

Mrs. V. is bemused, scratching her head, seemingly wondering what to do about me.

"Modicum, Modicum, Modicus!" she recites, seemingly casting a spell of caution, restraint, and moderation on me.

"My lost young soul, you need a strong remedy for the spirit. Sit down and I'll get you to read an antidote for the poison that is afflicting you at present."

With a blissful smile, she walks straight to a pile of huge, heavy books. She picks the one on top, brushes off the dust, and brings it to me. She then places it on my lap, sits by my side, opens the book right in the middle, and turns back two pages, then asks me to read...

"The Land of the Happy People"

Once upon a time,
in a land not so far from heaven,
there were quite a few happy people,
but many more angry ones.

And as there were more in numbers,
happiness was usually overcome by anger.

And this gave way to another awkward problem,
the happier the people got,
the angrier the other became.

Sometimes, it seemed like happiness
was not contagious enough.

For some, it seemed like anger
was the only thing that could be felt.

It all made up for
an absurd and hard to define world,
as the angry people
were uncomfortable with, even resentful of,
the permanent and unshakeable
sunny disposition and happiness of the others.

Was it a happy place dominated by anger?
or
Was it a place full of anger dominated by happiness?

Which one did really have the power?
Happiness or anger?
Could an angry person be happy?
Or even smile?
Was there any anger or pain in happiness?

Could anger and joy walk side by side?
Could there be joy
amongst adversity and tragedy?

Did angry people know how to be happy?
Did happy people know how to be angry?
Did angry people know what happiness was?
Did happy people know what anger was?
Was there a formula for how to be happy?

Once upon a time,
in a land not so far from heaven
there were quite a few happy people.
In the end, they prevailed
over the many other angry ones
and ended anger and sadness forevermore.

"Should I presume that you, Mrs. V., and I, are part of the happy people, and my mom, my teacher, and all of those other folks aren't?" I ask.

"For the moment, yes, but be careful, those angry individuals are everywhere, and they are like body snatchers that can grab you at any time. Also, be mindful of anger itself, as all alone, it can take over at any moment, poisoning your ability to be happy.

"My flustered mentee, ask yourself, why today of all days? Why did you notice anger in all those people? Why not yesterday or the day

before? After all, they all have the same personality every day of their lives. Besides, was it necessarily their anger what you detected, or perhaps just your own?"

Mrs. V. lets her words sink in and when they do, I look back at her with the big wide eyes of a boy in awe and wonder.

"You see how easy anger can get you. In this case, apparently, the anger of others. In short, my dear boy, it all depends on your attitude and the kind of life lenses you wear with which to contemplate and judge other people. Here is something else I want you to read about the paths we follow in life..."

"The Spinning Wheel of Life"

The spinning wheel of life
goes around and around,
that's why everything we see through,
comes and goes around, full circle,
to the place it started,
or where it ended.

Yes, in many ways life is a circle,
or better said,
a series of never-ending elliptical bends and curves,
of a bigger, wider circle.

And what seems new and unique to you,

it has indeed already happened!
Millions of times before!

Because you see…
with each turn of the wheel,
what was, what is, and what will be
are one in the same,
as in every one of life's turns,
there's a beginning,
then life takes us for a spin,
and then inevitably,
there is an end to everything.

But rejoice,
since the wheel endlessly spins,
an end is also a new beginning,
and as nothing stops, life is, therefore,
a constant, circular, flowing loop!
Spinning and spinning,
around and around,
what is, is,
what was, will be,
what will be, already was,
and will be again…

But above all,

let us rejoice now!
Especially of those we love,
and what we have,
whatever that is,
as we do not know,
when it will end.

But do not be distracted,
there are moments in one's life,
that start at the very end,
and others that end at the very beginning,
thus, it is sound and astute to remember,
that an opening always awaits us in life,
the start of a new beginning.

Let us then spin the wheel of life
around and around,
we'll go in circles,
where the beginning,
the end,
and the middle of everything
are one and the same,
just a different spin.

"Mrs. V., is my life a circle then?" I ask.

"Not exactly, think about your circles in life as the trajectory of the wake you leave behind as you live," Mrs. V. replies, "So, my obfuscated mentee, everything comes around full circle in life. In the end, we either draw well-lived and rounded circles or not, thus you may as well strive to be happy, to live a gentle, blissful, and inspired life, always following the better instincts of your heart. But young lad, those are subjects that we will visit sometime down the road of your tutelage."

Professor Cromwell-Smith ends his class by drawing a circle in the air with two fingers joined together, and this is followed by many of the students who spiritedly emulate their inspirational time traveller. It is a simple moment for a mesmerized group of students drawing circles in the air as a symbol of a strong emotional connection with the professor and his class. And from then onwards, the circles in the air morph into a ritual that in turn becomes a parting or a greeting gesture among many of them.

"I'll see you all next week so we can continue our journey into past moments of my life, with poetry as our inspirational telescope. Class dismissed."

Professor Cromwell-Smith lets his last words linger and then his class wraps up with seemingly countless circles in the air.

Chapter 7

Hope

Today, New England has awoken to a regional state of emergency, as the night prior the tail end of a hurricane brushed the region's coastline. Many communities have been devastated. Many families are now homeless.

Professor Cromwell-Smith is soaking wet as he navigates his bicycle through the light but steady rain and the mildly flooded campus streets, caused by the previous night's storm.

As he enters the main building, everything inside, as well as in the classroom, appears to be wet. Floors, umbrellas, raincoats; there is wetness all around.

"Things are quite messy out there," the professor admits in earnest.

"Today, in light of the tragedy that is afflicting our state I, and I am sure some of you as well, will go back to a moment in time where hope was the last thing I gave up on."

Over the last six months, my parents have been helping me apply to every conceivable university in England, France, and Switzerland. But, in spite of my stellar academic record, one by one, rejections have been flooding in. My parents' initial confidence, that I initially adopted as well, has been dealt a setback and has been progressively eroded blow by blow. So, talk of technical school or

apprenticeship has begun to emerge here and there, during their nightly fights of blame. Today is Tuesday and I know exactly where I want to go, or should I say, where I need to go. And no one is better in dire moments than Mr. M., the Equilibrist.

On this foggy, misty day, the Morris-Rose and Sons antique bookstore is swarming with people and vehicles. From a distance, I can see a couple of TV trucks and cameramen as they load their equipment. A dozen or so people exit the bookshop, some with mics, others with headsets. Then, within ten minutes, the street corner is back to normal and as empty as its daily usual self, that's when I make my grand entrance, which is anything but that, just a facade, as again, I am not noticed at all. Mr. M. is busy on the phone, taking notes. His body language reflects his stress. I sit at my favorite corner and watch him get progressively angrier until he hangs up, returning the handset to its cradle just short of slamming it. Then he huffs and puffs while slowly calming down. It takes a while for him to come to his senses, and finally, my presence catches his attention.

"Not a good day, Erasmus," he sighs.

I begin to stand up as he continues.

"Sit, sit, I did not mean to drive you away. I always have time for you. Mentoring is a labor of love that never ceases."

I hesitate and, for a moment, don't know what to do.

"Erasmus, you are not here today just for reading. Something is troubling you; your eyes are lost and clamoring for tutelage."

"Indeed," I reply.

"What's troubling you?"

"Every university is turning me down."

"That's surprising given your academic records. Do not worry, my son, you've earned it, and eventually several of those academic institutions will gladly welcome you. Keep in mind. You and your parents are aiming high, as you want to go to the best there is in higher education, which is quite a feat. Paraphrasing Machiavelli, 'There is very little space in the upper rooms of the palace,' especially when a scholarship is involved."

He paces the room, finally makes up his mind, and walks briskly to the far end of the main hall. On top of the table, there is a green and gold book of average size. He picks it up and, by the time he reaches me, the book is already opened to the chosen page. He then sits next to me while speaking.

"My tormented and gifted mentee, let me read to you something very special about the profoundness of hope and why it is such a powerful source of strength."

"Hope"

When things couldn't be worse or direr,
when all our strengths and fortitudes are gone,
hope is what always pulls us through.

Hope is how we outlast adversity
and overcome every and any obstacle.

Hope is the life vest for our spirit and soul.

Hope is always our passport to freedom
from the shackles of our mind
and the chains of hardship.

When there is Hope
we are not afraid of being afraid
and there is simply no fear of fear itself.
Hope is always our safe-conduct
to the land of endurance and resilience,
hope is always the seed of courage.
Hope is one of the most powerful tools
to survive and make it through the game of life.
Hope is that calming and steady inner power
that dotes us with bountiful confidence
and steely resolve.

When there is hope we are always ready
to restart, rebuild, recreate, restore, renew,
rekindle, repeat, rely, redo, and remake it all
over and over and over again.

When we hope, we are never willing to give up.

Hope in oneself and others,
cures blindness and deafness in our soul and spirit,

filling life with shining lights,
whispering tunes and melodies
on seemingly non-existent paths
and non-existent doors.
Hope is our secret elixir for a life with purpose.
Hope is the well of will from which we draw,
to find meaning while we are alive.

By being true to ourselves,
while we hope, we always remain authentic.

Hope makes us feel invincible
against the most devastating weather systems.
Hope allows us to face the eye of any storm
without blinking.
Hope equips us with stealth armor
underneath soft gentle silk.
Hope enables us to always get back up
and to never, ever, stay down.

We hope when we stubbornly believe
we can make our future better,
and not only do we know what we hope for,
but the degree to which we can do so.

Thus, we hope when our determination
is more powerful

than any circumstance, or anyone we may be facing,
or any place in life's journey we may be at.

Hope feels great deep inside our core,
and that is why it easily spreads to others.

When we hope, we deliberately choose
to adopt a positive, resolute behavior,
that is why hope is most enduring
when along the way,
we knock away all emotional roadblocks
from its path.

Hope is far stronger
when we hope not only for our own wellbeing,
but for that of our loved ones as well.

When we hope, we stubbornly believe
there is always a solution
and a way in or out of anything.

When we hope against the tides
in spite of what oppresses and wounds us,
and when we hope with the belief
that the sacred and spiritual
far transcend the mundane,
then, hope morphs into an existential shield

80

against failure, quitting or surrender,
then, hope morphs into an existential weapon
against pessimism or defeat.

Hope is a virtuous, elevated state of life
that exalts our human condition
and strengthens our character.

Hope's main virtue is
that it makes us perennially resilient.

Hope's most powerful ammunition
is courage.

Hope is what builds and defines us
as 'life warriors',
ready to overcome and endure.

Hope is the ultimate exercise there is
in self-determination,
and when there is no other one left,
it is the last liberty standing,
enabling us to choose,
regardless of anything and anyone,
to have a better future ahead of us.

"Erasmus, hope is your best source of strength and freedom."

"Mr. M., is this then how I'll never give up on anything?" I ask.

"Well, impetuous apprentice, there are times in life when you'll have to let go. This time though is totally different, as hope should be your natural attitude to begin with. Thus, when you go after something, do it with passion, but always driven by the strength and resolve that hope gives you. So, it is not that you never give up, it is that you never lose hope, and therefore never give up.

"You've fixed my day. Each time the media rains down on our little town to tell their audience the same old story again about our countless antique book shops, they have this nagging habit of wanting to interview me, of all people. I simply cannot tolerate the sheer ignorance of the journalists they send over here."

He speaks with a relaxed smile. As I leave, I have no longer any doubt that he is right. I will be accepted, eventually, into one of the few upper rooms of the palace.

Professor Cromwell-Smith brings the class back by reminding everyone that there are always new beginnings in life, moments that test our core, while hope always sits at the center of those crossroads as our safe-conduct to a better life.

"Professor, why is hope the last freedom standing?" asks a bespectacled Japanese girl.

"Because even in the face of great tragedy and hardship, through the loss of everyone and everything, nothing or no one can deprive you of your ability to hope," he replies.

Total silence follows as the professor seems to be looking at everyone straight in the eye while panning through the audience. His stare is serene and resolute; a man possessed by hope.

"Have a nice day everyone."

Then, as the students leave, one after another continue to glance back and forth at the professor with eyes of gratitude and discovery.

There is hope after all, he ponders as he approaches his old rusty bike.

Chapter 8

To Be Inspired

Today, the faculty has been magnanimous with Professor Cromwell-Smith, as a mid-size auditorium has been made available for his class. It seats more than two hundred students.

"How's everyone today?" he asks.

The room is designed in an IMAX kind of way, almost as if the professor is speaking to every student face to face.

The room is packed, then, and the humming, buzzing, and rumbling of the crowd grows. He nods his head in response to their enthusiasm. He is also humbled by their presence, as poetry rarely draws this kind of crowd.

"Allow me today to take you back into a moment in time when I was consumed by fear."

As my 18th birthday approaches, I am full of doubts about my future. I am about to leave my home and live away from my parents for the first time in my life. Being accepted by Oxford was thrilling, but the feeling lasted just a few weeks. My parents drove me to the beautiful city and university, and it was exhilarating. I loved every minute of it, but a couple of days later the jitters came back, even stronger than before.

As I walk into Mr. Newton-Paine's shop, I am in search of advice and support. Fear is taking hold of me as my departure date approaches. Then, as I come in, my fearless mentor is waving off an old lady visiting from Liverpool.

"Good morning to you, my dear young man," he says.

"I need your counsel, Mr. Newton."

"You do look like you are in need of it, Erasmus. What is it? I am all yours."

"I'm lacking determination. I am anxious and afraid. What should I do? I want to do well at Oxford, but I am not certain that I am ready for it."

Tilting his head forward, my humble hero looks at me through his glasses, perched on the end of his nose. I can feel his mind working, pondering the choices as he limps away and pulls out a scroll from a shelf filled with them. He pulls down the bottom side of a rolled manuscript and extends the page in front of him, holding the top and bottom ends of the scribble to keep it open, and placing it on his lecturing podium.

"All you need to find, young scholar, is inspiration, and the contents of this scroll will help you find the wisdom for seeking and treasuring inspiration in life."

He then starts to read, and his very first words enrapture and hypnotize me...

"An Inspired Life"

To be inspired is
to be continuously and blissfully happy,
to inhale deeply and feel really, really, good
as we sigh in joy to the sweet taste
of purely and simply being alive.

Living an inspired life is a gift, a magic incantation
that makes us life sorcerers,
the kind that asks for nothing,
but dispense wizardry back in spades.

Behind an inspired person, there is always
that something or someone that starts it all
and that we connect so profoundly with.

Around an inspired person, there is always
a powerful halo of positive energy,
a magnetic field
that not only draws from our best talents,
but also attracts endless virtuous circles.

When we are inspired,
we are dressed in a mantle of immutability.
A permanent twinkle in our smile.

Eyes filled with the peace and calmness
of a full life.

When we are inspired, we contemplate life,
through a magical magnifying glass as a rosy picture,
even in the most trying of circumstances,
That is why,
to be inspired requires
a great deal of ingenuity.

When we are inspired, all our best attributes
are always on call,
ifs, buts, or can'ts are not in the picture
and there are no limits, boundaries, or periscopes,
but wide and open horizons
for the countless moon shots ahead of us.

For an inspired person, anything and everything is possible
as opportunities that lies in waiting
to be tapped, discovered, or made.

It is a chance, an unsculpted rock,
an uncrafted melody, an unwritten verse,
an intimate and unpainted masterpiece
yet to be born.

To live an inspired life is
to be in a state of readiness
to capture the best life has to offer,
to squeeze the most out of our journey.

It is when life as a whole is fertile ground
for our dreams, fantasies, and imagination,
and with all our good antennae up,
we acquire a noble altered state,
hypersensitive to anything worth pursuing.

When we are inspired,
there is no burden, drag, or heaviness,
and everything becomes light, bright, and inviting.
Everything feels effortless.

Will moves mountains,
inspiration while doing so,
recreates them.

That's why inspiration renders will ordinary,
supersedes passion and conviction,
and reduces self-confidence to a simple tool.

Sometimes inspiration hits us like a thunderbolt,
for some, it's simply a state,

a condition of sublime desire,
Sometimes to be inspired
is to be moved by heaven and driven by angels,
For some others it's to be provoked by the soul
and sparkled by the spirit,
but inspiration is always tuned and honed
by our hearts.

When we are inspired,
we invent,
we create,
we tinker,
we build,
we craft,
we art,
we solve,
we visualize,
we foresee,
we explain,
we understand,
we explore,
we seek,
we study,
we pray,
we love,
we try and try and try,

we give back,

we do,

we make

and therefore, we live in full.

Inspiration is the stuff of wizards,

life wizards that hover through it.

To be inspired,

to live an inspired life

and to be an inspired person

is to be continuously and blissfully happy.

A kind of happiness

where we are permanently grateful to life.

A kind of happiness

we continuously pay back.

A kind of inspired happiness

that never goes away.

"Erasmus, take stock of your life and realize how happy you are. You've grown up surrounded by love. Right on your doorstep lies a world that matches your passions, in which you've been immersed from an early age, and now, to top it all, this wonderful new horizon has opened for you at Oxford, one of the best academic institutions in the world. Don't stand in your own way. Now is the time for you to spread your wings and fly. Seize the moment and grab what life

is offering you by the horns, addressing whatever is rattling you from within. Go for it with all your heart. At the same time, be grateful and capture every moment and everything that is offered to you, especially all that you earn through hard work," smiles Mr. N. encouragingly.

He continues, "To be inspired is a state, a condition to which you are driven, with grace and nobility, by a sublime and overwhelming desire to live, to make, and to be happy. Inspiration harnesses all your best gifts into a highly functional state that brings out the absolute best in you. Erasmus, you should pursue inspiration in your life, as it will provide you with continuous happiness."

Later that night, as I stroll back home, I can feel life's air through my lungs. Slowly, at first, my stride and gait start to change, then my face rictus as well. By the time I walk into my house, a thousand thoughts have clicked inside of me. My mum then notes that for the first time in weeks my face shows a broad smile and steely resolute eyes.

"And that's a wrap," declares the professor.

The large auditorium is filled with dreamy looks. Most attendees seem like they are not there, but rather traveling to faraway places within themselves. Then, as Professor Cromwell-Smith watches them leave, he sighs with deep satisfaction at the involuntary reflexive actions of the departing crowd, as many, if not all, keep on taking deep breaths, enjoying as they inhale that moment in their lives, seemingly tasting what it is to be inspired.

Chapter 9

Letting Go of the Past

Professor Cromwell-Smith has awakened this morning with a blinding headache. It started the previous evening and did not ease up throughout the night. There is no time to waste.

Treat each day as if it is your last, he reminds himself.

Then, as he pedals steadily through the empty streets, the pain begins to subside, and he knows exactly what it is he is going to reminisce about with his students on this day.

"Class, today I'll take you to a moment in time when I learned to use the power of the present as a key tool for dealing with grudges."

On my second visit home, I feel the urge to seek Mrs. V.'s words of love and wisdom. So, with great trepidation, I walk straight from the train station to her shop, and right as I walk in, suitcase in hand, she sees me and smiles. Then, in rapid short steps, she comes over and hugs me tightly against her chest. For the first time in weeks, I feel safe and protected. Then, as I start to relax, her inquisitive eyes already know there is something wrong.

"My dear boy, what has brought you here before going home, what's troubling you?" she asks.

"Mrs. V., how can I deal with resentment?"

"Are you holding any grudges, young Oxford student?"

"Not me, but a couple of fellows do against me." I reply.

"Why?"

"Oxford traditions, in one case. A girl, in another."

"Well, you can't control what others feel or how they behave. Each person writes their own life pages, day by day, in indelible ink on a book that is entirely theirs. But I do have a little something that bluntly depicts the futility of not letting go, of getting stuck in the past and not being able to move on."

She turns around and pulls out a thin grey and white book with gold-coated pages around the edges. She flips it open and lets me read.

"The Past and the Future"

Conventional wisdom is that,
when you do the wrong thing,
eventually, the past catches up with you
and holds you accountable.

But there is also
the unspoken truth that,
when we fail to do in the present
what we are supposed to,
when we do not harness the power of now,
we are just postponing life itself,
and the future will eventually
catch up to us, as well.

And we may not like it,
as it does not belong to us,
because we did not build or create it.

While we won't own it, it will own us.

So, we should ask ourselves,
are we postponing life?
Do we keep pushing it forward?
The future is coming!
It is just around the corner
and when it finally arrives,
we may be stuck with it!
Until we start building our future
one day at a time
now!
Then we'll own it,
then and only then,
the future will be ours.

"Mrs. V., what is the difference between the past and the future catching up with you?" I ask.

"One catches up with you for things you did, the other for the things you failed to do."

"Erasmus, you need to treasure and learn from your past, but never be a slave to it. Too many of us live 'ever after' consumed by things *that no longer exist, things that are otherwise long gone, but still linger in the tortuous, masochist, and narrow, very narrow corridors and labyrinths of our minds," Mrs. V. advises.*

She continues animatedly, "You must live now! Do not skip a day, do not push forward what you can do today, but do it free from negative fantasies left behind in the past."

I ponder this for a moment, and proceed to ask, "But what about if moving on is not enough to cure a grudge?"

"My young inquisitor, I have right here the best antidote there is for wicked thoughts, a poisoned spirit, and an angry heart. Read right here, my dear boy..."

"Reach Out"

Lend a hand
Share a dream
Join in hope
Pray for others
Extend a favor
Give a kiss
Hug each other
Teach those in need
Learn from the wise
Take nothing
Always forgive
Use the strength of the truth

Love with passion
Remember your friends
Practice the power of humility
Shine on one another
Wait with grace and patience
Gift in earnest
Receive in gratitude
Live with others
Give into someone else's heart
Reach out, reach out to life

"So, is it all about giving?"

"To cure a poisoned spirit and an angry heart stuck in the past, absolutely yes! My precious mentee, holding grudges will keep you stuck in the past in endless loops of pain. When you give, you should always do so despite the behavior of others, as it'll make your deeds not only genuine, but it'll also allow you independence. As your actions won't be conditioned by how others respond to you."

Professor Cromwell-Smith's class keeps growing and today they have moved to an even larger auditorium that is set to be their permanent oversized classroom. As the students leave, it is obvious to many that their teacher looks frail and tired, as he waves everyone off sitting behind his desk, something he never does. He, in turn, seems about to faint but is able to keep it together until everybody is gone, at which point he finally lets go, slumping headfirst on his

97

desk. The heavy thump is the last noise heard in the large hall for quite a while.

Chapter 10

Winning and Self-Reliance

It's been two weeks since Professor Cromwell-Smith was rushed to the hospital after having been found by a diligent night security guard.

His head shaved, ashen skin color, and dark shadows under his eyes are confirmation of the widespread rumor.

Yes, he tells himself as he walks into a standing applause. *The secret is out.*

The faces he sees cheering are expressing support, respect, relief, and joy to see him act again.

Everyone knows that you are sick, he quietly scolds himself.

"Thank you, thank you all... Have a seat please," requests the professor.

With trepidation, but not acting consciously, the young woman with curly blond hair sits down in the back of the room. She feels ambivalent about the rabbit hole into which she is falling but can't quite control the intensity of the draw the professor's story is having on her.

"Today I'll refer to a period in my life when I started playing competitive sports and was confronted for the first time with the culture of winning or losing. Little did I know then, how valuable those lessons were going to be, enabling me to deal with and overcome the life challenges that I face now. It starts like this..."

"Will he still be open or not?" I ask myself over and over again as I ride the late afternoon train back home.

Then, an hour later, as we cross the border between England and Wales, I mumble aloud about the subject I've been obsessing on over the last few days.

"Rowing or rugby, or neither?"

Those are the choices that I have. Later as I walk the empty streets of my hometown, I reason that, since I have been raised in the world of books, the adrenaline rush, and the desire to compete are foreign to me. I desperately need my fearless war hero's wisdom.

That is why the very first thing I'm doing upon arrival on this short visit from Oxford is heading straight to his place. Then, I feel an immense sense of relief when I turn the corner and see the lights emanating from his shop, the only ones on both sides of the street. Knowing his habits for so many years has made me guess right that he would be open.

"Mr. Newton, it is so nice to see you," I say, smiling.

"Come on over, dear boy; let me give you a hug."

He stands up with difficulty and as he swings his way to me, I see it. "I fell a few weeks ago," he says, quickly pre-empting me as he lifts the shiny wooden cane to point it out. "Now that you see that our physical attributes are fleeting, even for former gifted athletes like me, may I know what brings you here at this late hour? Surely there is an important reason."

"Mr. N., I don't know if I've got what it takes to compete. At Oxford, that is something one constantly runs into. I don't have the fire in my belly to do it. I don't see the point or the thrill of it at all, and it worries me that I may fail because of it."

Newton-Paine smiles broadly knowing in an instant there is a literary prescription for his mentee.

"Come on, help me," I plead.

I walk alongside him until we are standing in front of a locked two by two box that contains an enormous book, which through the security glass seems quite old. Mr. N. punches in the code and the door opens.

"Erasmus, please carefully slide the book out by pulling the small rug underneath it," requests Mr. N., guiding me.

Then, using the bookmarker cord, he delicately opens the book exactly to where he wants.

"My reluctant competitor, this old and precious book contains the kind of wisdom that you are looking for. Let me read it to you..."

"Winning is not for the Faint of Heart"

The road to victory is a game of survival. It is war.
You visualize yourself as a gladiator in the arena,
a stealth ninja warrior ready to attack
in the shadows,
a bullfighter facing the fury of the beast.
You see yourself choosing

between winning and losing
as if they were life or death.

You win when you want it so badly
that it hurts inside.
You win when you want it so much more
than your opponent does.

You win when your mindset is that nothing,
except your values,
can stop you from achieving success.
You win when your sole purpose
is to defeat your opponents.
You win by simultaneously playing your strengths
and your adversaries' weaknesses
or simply by flat-out outworking them.

You win when, deliberately and quietly,
you try to capture each one
of your opponent's strengths and virtues.

You win when in your opponent's eyes,
you are fierce and steadfast
in your game plan and execution,
and yet, discreetly tweak and adapt
in a split second.

You win when, in preparation for a contest,
you approach every task with tunnel vision
and such steely resolve
that nothing or no one is able
to prevent you from completing it,
because 'the art of winning' can only be mastered
by 'paying every due' and 'burning every candle.'
Preparing to be ready to win is a long road
that must be travelled in its entirety.

You win when you are one step ahead
of your opponent
and still ask yourself, can I do it better?

You win when unflappable,
you 'keep on' going back
time and again to knock on the same door
previously slammed in your face.

You win when a 'no' is nothing
but an invitation to try again,
You win when you are totally and utterly oblivious
to the word 'rejection.'

You win when you know how to seek,

take advice, and learn from those
who know how to win.

You win when you take on the better side
of your ego and make it
your friend, your ally, and your weapon,
because as opposed to the shallowness
and narcissism of arrogance,
self-confidence derives
from knowledge and experience,
and is therefore unshakeable.

You win when through discipline and perseverance
you acquire the knowledge and experience
that provides you with the self-confidence needed
to master whatever you want to be the best at.

You win when you can use your anger
as a source of strength,
when you morph your rage
into a burning and unstoppable desire
and when you draw from your 'well of will,'
the fire and the fury needed to win.

You only win when you've experienced
countless losses, defeats, stumbles, and fumbles,

and the worse they have been,
the better prepared you are to win in the future.
But for a path to victory
one must harness one's very own demons,
one must "rein in" a unique cast of 'free-spirited' characters
that inhabit the kingdoms of our mind and spirit.

That's why, in order to win we have to
conquer our own mountains,
break down our own walls,
vanquish enemy armies,
annihilate pessimists,
ridicule skeptics,
render mute the excusers and naysayers,
exile the slouches,
calm the fearful, making them our allies
and turn the doubters into charlatans,
and we have to do it all
within the confines of ourselves,
as we do it when in battle.

Sometimes winning requires you to follow
your gut, your better fibers,
your most animalistic, atavistic,
and primal instincts,
all shaken and stirred into

105

a cocktail of raw passion.

Sometimes winning requires you
to follow your brain,
your rational thinking,
your battle plans, strategy, and logic.

Often you require both!
Even though on any given Sunday,
in the game of winning,
passion generally beats brains!

You win when you enjoy and share
the spoils from the act of winning.
You win when you live, appreciate and value
the journey to victory.
You win when it brings out the best in you,
you win when it makes you better,
when you win, you celebrate life.

But above all,
you win when you are not fooled by it,
but to the contrary,
always keep it in its right place, as winning,
even though an essential component of life,
is only a 'game of life.'

It is not existential or sacred
but mundane and passing.
It is not love or friendship, neither truth nor faith,
nor virtue or values,
but only a 'will and grit' booster, a worthy test
of the intensity with which you live your life.

But winning is not for the faint of heart
as it requires courage and strength.

Winning is for those that challenge life
with their hearts
and for whom living a life in full inexorably includes
winning as an intrinsically part of the equation,
to squeeze out of life the sublime passion of victory.

"So, Mr. N., I don't necessarily win against an opponent?" I ask.
"That's right, human beings are not always the adversary. Life is filled with obstacles, challenges, difficulties even tragedies, some of them seemingly insurmountable, that only the attitude of a winner can defeat," Mr. N. clarifies.
"Bottom line, you are telling me that I need to know how to win to be able to navigate the perils of life."
"Right on, right on, my boy. You need an indomitable desire and will to triumph. It is a key ingredient to be able to withstand and conquer whatever life throws at you or whatever you set your sights

on. But my maturing apprentice, there is an additional gift in this 20th century book that will infuse you with additional wisdom to be a doer, a maker, and a wholesome life warrior."

Mr. N. then parts the book, placing its second marking cord, exactly where he wants, and starts to read with a resolve even greater than the previous reading.

"Self-Reliance"

*Self-reliance is the action and life
of self-assertiveness.*

It is being accountable first and foremost to oneself.

*It is the realization that I can rely on myself
before anyone or anything,
And even though out of reasons of
love, generosity, a moral imperative,
or a combination of any of them,
I can put others before or ahead of me
in my life's endeavors.*

*When it comes to dependence though,
I depend firstly on myself
before I depend on others,
as I shall never expect, count, or rely on others*

to act instead of me.
For what I am supposed to do,
what only I can do,
what only I should do,
by myself?

Also, I rely on myself and what I believe in,
irrespective and above what others believe.

As I rely on myself first,
I am immune to the opinions
and influence of others.

I rely on myself despite what society thinks.

I rely on my instincts and my gut,
not instead,
but before any norm, rule, or law.
As I rely on myself, I break away,
inoculate against or do not fall into
the chains of conformism, indoctrination,
the annihilation, or disappearance of myself.

I rely on myself first
as it is the only way I can establish
my individuality, my character, my personality,

in other words, my own self.

I rely on myself first because
it's the foundation of my independence
And the seed of
my sense of self-worth, self-respect, and dignity.

If I can govern myself
without the help or influence of anyone,
then I have acquired all of the above.

I will rely on myself first if I think, feel, and act
with integrity, without impulsiveness, and according
to my spiritual, moral/ethical, and family values.

I rely on myself first because I trust myself,
and, as a result, believe and have self-confidence
to face life as me and not as someone else,
true to my identity
with all my capacities and talents.

"Young Erasmus, don't expect or even desire that anything will be handed easily to you in life. Just hold on firmly to the belief that you must earn it."

"You mean that caring and having empathy for others is something that I could decide to pour my heart into, but its foundations will

originate only from my own self-reliance," I say, attempting to clarify.

"Spot on, my boy, spot on. Self-reliance and individualism are often confused with being selfish. Actually, self-reliant people, even as they depend on themselves first, can still be fully dedicated to helping others in need. Self-reliance or depending on oneself is not incompatible at all with giving," Mr. N. concludes.

I stare at the World War II pilot for a long time, absorbing the power and the wisdom of what he has shared with me today.

Professor Cromwell-Smith's voice feels weak and hoarse. He wraps up the class.

"But Professor, I do rely on others all the time," says an African American student.

"Of course, you do, but you must rely on yourself first."

Professor Cromwell-Smith lets the words sink in before waving the students off until the following week.

"Have a nice day, guys. See you next week."

A couple of his students stay behind and walk him all the way to his bike. Then, as he leaves pedaling without much balance, they are all thinking the same thing: *How long is he going to last?*

Chapter 11

The Importance of Small Details in Life

Professor Cromwell-Smith is feeling a lot better today. His aggressive tumor is shrinking. He is fully aware that it is a miracle to be the beneficiary of a state-of-the-art treatment that has already saved the life of a former U.S. President.

Treat each day as if it is your last, he reminds himself once more, as he parks his old rusty bike alongside a dozen others.

Surrounded by the hues of spring, he feels inspired to talk about that bittersweet period of his life when he discovered love. Minutes later, that's how he begins his class.

"One of the great mysteries in life is the unexpected bends in the road, some of them for the worst but others for the better, and for the latter, we should always be grateful, as those are unforeseen gifts. There was a moment in my life when a lightning bolt hit me allowing for an epiphany. From that moment forward my life has never been the same."

Not quite four months into my master's degree, I fly home for a week to join my parents on their 25th wedding anniversary. But once over there, I can't wait to meet with Mrs. V. There is so much I have to share with her. That's how within hours after my arrival, I rush to visit my beloved mentor. After fifteen minutes of pure joy and an outpouring of spontaneous affection from my effusive cheerleader,

113

I can't hold it in any longer and start to earnestly share everything with her.

"Mrs. V., ever since I saw her for the first time, all I can do is..." I falter.

The knot in my throat chokes me and I feel overwhelmed by a torrent of feelings and emotions.

"How can you love someone you've never met?" I ask both myself and Mrs. V.

"Tell me about her. Tell me, dear boy," she says encouragingly.

"It happened on my second weekend at Harvard, just before a football game, as the marching band approached, their baton twirler caught my attention. She not only had amazing dexterity, but also an intense yet joyous energy, and the most beautiful pair of eyes I've ever seen. Her huge and infectious smile made me chuckle as I wished it would never end. This incredibly wonderful magnetism seized and engulfed me, and I have not been in control of my heart ever since."

"And what did you do about it?" she asks with dreamy eyes.

"Nothing. I was simply frozen. I could not take my eyes off her as I followed her every move, even from afar. They disbanded and put their things away, but I stood still as if paralyzed."

"And then?"

"This was three months ago. Now I know everything about her, and she even accidentally introduced herself in a brief encounter, but otherwise, I've done nothing, I don't know what to do. I am paralyzed by fear," I admit.

"Erasmus, there is no prescribed formula for love, much less for how or whom you love, or even when you love."

Mrs. V. paces back and forth, hand on her chin, as she makes up her mind.

"In matters of love, wisdom can be our guiding light. It sprinkles our instincts, our feelings, and our passions like a love compass. It answers countless love crossword puzzles that we may have to solve," she says, emanating with knowledge.

Then she picks up a small book that she obviously keeps handy from one of her desk shelves.

"Here is one of them, hopefully, it will steer you into action in the pursuit of your infatuation. Read here please, my dear..."

"The Better Instincts of our Hearts"

*There are things in life that
we can only do from our hearts
and those we never regret.*

*In fact, we'll do them
over and over again,
the same exact way.*

*These are acts of life
which we draw
from the better instincts of our hearts,*

are driven mainly
by passion, convictions, and principles,
self-interest or consequences don't matter
as much as one's beliefs,
for that someone
whom,
we are ready to take a bullet for.

One thing is absolutely certain,
these types of monumental steps
are not driven by our brains!
We would never have
the courage and unselfishness
to hurt ourselves
or act against our own best interests,
as both are exclusively matters of the heart.

These acts of valor are
where heroes are born,
the course of history is changed,
lives are spared or saved
and humanity shines and rises,
to its highest levels.

There are many of us who are born
with great instincts of mind,

and there are also many of us who come to life
with great instincts of the heart,
but one of life's paradoxes
is that we always seem to follow
those instincts on which we are the weakest,
inevitably leading us
into unfulfilled and depressing lives.

And in matters of love,
brain and heart are oil and water,
they don't mix well,
because the brain cannot
create, govern, control, or sustain love
nor vice-versa.

When we follow
the better instincts of our brains
in matters of love,
there is no love,
but rather thoughts instead of feelings.

What likely there is,
is an arrangement where we settle
for comfort and emptiness.

Because inasmuch as

the better instincts of our minds
serve us well,
when logic, convenience,
and common sense are required,
when we look back at life,
we will always realize that
immense, absolute, and wholesome happiness
only comes to us
when we have followed
the better instincts of our hearts.

"In this short visit to Wales, young man, the message you are getting from this old lady that loves you dearly, is to always follow your heart," Mrs. V. smiles.

"Okay, okay, I get it. But how do I go about it? What to do, Mrs. V.?" I ask eagerly.

"Well, perhaps you can start by understanding what being blissful is all about. If you do, I'm certain that you'll be able to act on your feelings, while you're in possession of precious knowledge of perhaps one of the most important hidden treasures in matters of love."

Mrs. V. pages through the same beautiful book and hands it to me already opened to the right page.

"Read over here, my lovelorn mentee..."

"Life is Bliss (The Importance of Little Details in Life)"

If you want to live a blissful life,
pay attention to the little details,
both in the receiving and giving ends.

But not the kind where 'the devil is in the... ',
as those are easy and hide in plain sight
and are usually expected
rules, norms, or stipulations
that we either follow, ignore, break, or circumvent.

So, they are narrow in human nature
and binary in their scope,
as they simply bite you or they don't.

No, to live a life in bliss you must pay attention
to a different kind of little details,
those that are gestures of love,
those that come straight from the heart.
They are usually spontaneous and unexpected,
often hold very little or no material value,
but always provide immense bliss and joy,
the kind when it is hard to breathe
in the throats of both the dispenser and the recipient
as emotions bundle up in a knot.

These types of little details require genial creativity,
but that becomes easy when propelled
by overwhelming empathy and caring for others.

When we receive little details,
they hold their biggest value,
when we are richer, in health,
and things are better, well and good,
yet we are still humble enough to pay attention,
to appreciate and value
how much we are loved by others.

When we give,
the little details in life have their greatest worth,
when we are poorer, in sickness
and things are at their worst,
not good or simply bad,
yet we still have the heart and the desire
to give to others whom we care about.

It is on those extremes,
valuing what we are offered when we don't need it,
or caring about giving the very little we have left,
when little details in life matter the most,
become unforgettable, never leave
and stay with us forever.

Life is bliss when caught by surprise,
overcome by emotion
we hide our faces behind the palms of our hands,
when we find that little note left in our pocket,
leave that flower on her pillow,
or in those tiny precious gestures that mom, dad,
granny, and grandpa never forget,
those little things that never fail to be there,
that supportive hug or kiss,
that reassuring or uplifting smile,
that contagious laughter,
those calming, maybe loving,
perhaps tender and grateful eyes,
any or all those little things
that make us react in bliss:
What a gesture, they love me.
Oh my, I love him, her, them, you...
with all my heart.

So, if you want to live life in bliss,
pay close attention to the little details in life,
those that come straight from the heart,
those that are spontaneous gestures of love,
those that are just little things,
those that we offer and receive with absolute joy,
those that we never forget for the rest of our lives.

121

"Erasmus, love grows up out of little things, love is captured through small gestures," Mrs. V. says softly. "Love is preserved and made of teeny, tiny details that we give and take, to and from one another."

At that moment, I realize that for the first time in my life I feel what it is to be blissful.

She continues, "Focus on giving with all your heart, but mind very carefully who you are giving to, as what makes little details resonate, is their catalyst, empathy."

Professor Cromwell-Smith flashes a huge smile as he wraps up his class. He sees curious, expectant looks all around, so he reacts accordingly.

"Yes, yes. The answer is yes, in our next class we will dive deeper into this chapter of my life," he declares.

As each session takes place and the story moves forward, it all resonates more and more with her. What started as vaguely familiar, becomes inexorably real to the young woman with the curly blond hair.

Chapter 12

Falling in Love

It is early morning, and the heat is already omnipresent. Today, Professor Cromwell-Smith's pedaling cadence is deliberately slow, and his body language is seemingly calm, even pensive. Yet inside, he is a whirlwind of emotions, revisiting places of the heart long buried, but never erased. The intensity of it all has him completely unsettled as a torrent of unearthed feelings keeps on bursting forward flooding every inch of his living self.

Soon thereafter, he walks into the auditorium. A crowd hungry for more awaits him.

"Isn't this insanely awesome?" he asks a smiling and nodding audience.

"Dear friends, bear with me today as we traverse this phase of my life together. Please forgive me if I become a tad emotional. These are feelings that I, or any of us, can't simply rationalize. All right, here we go," the professor says, inhaling deeply, nostrils flared, eyes already lost in the past.

It's been three weeks since I wrote to Mrs. V. and shared with her the joy and, yes, the bliss of having found the love of my life. I thanked her a million times.

Dear Mrs. V.,

I want to share the news with you, I'm madly in love and we're both utterly happy. Dearest Mrs. V., I won her heart through little gestures, I did! Little details that awed her heart. You are not going to believe this, her name is… well I call her Vicky, Vicky as in Victoria! Isn't it awesome? You both share the same name. I am certain that it's a good omen. Victoria. Victoria Emerson-Lloyd is her name, and we've been inseparable for the last eleven months.

Mrs. V., let me caution you that I am no poet nor writer. Nevertheless, I enclose here a couple of verses that I wrote to her and want to share with you. The first one shows exactly how I feel about her.

"Love's Rabbit Hole"

How do you know when love is knocking
at your door?

How do you know when it has arrived?
And its music, the music of angels,
is all out there waiting for you.

How do you know that whoever has reached you,
is maybe that travel mate
you've been wishing for, all along?

And how do you know if it's the right time,
right there and then,
to come out of your shell,
knocking down your protective shields?

You know it, because when that someone unexpectedly
irrupts into your life's journey,
it simply takes your breath away.

You know it,
when you can finally catch your breath
all you inhale feels at that moment
like there is absolutely
nothing else you would like to be doing,
nor anyone else in the world
you would like to be with,
other than your rabbit.

You know it as the world around you disappears
and you willingly fall
through the most scintillatious rabbit hole
you'll ever find in your life.

You know it when out of the blue,
the object of your desire

can't do or say anything wrong,
as all you see is perfection
through benevolent magnifying glasses
made of boundless candor,
ingenuity, and romance.

You know it, when from the get-go,
you feel comfortable, confident,
and light on your feet,
and life becomes a journey of two,
impregnated with magic,
happiness, passion, and joy.

You know it because you become possessed
with this inexplicable certainty
that you are safe, protected, and never alone.

And you know it when you see yourself
visualizing your life, your future, your family, and your children,
only with your other half.

And you know it because love's rabbit hole
is one from which you'll never want to climb out.

Mrs. V., Vicky is lively and bubbly. She is fun and foolish. Loves to dress in blue. Quite fitting indeed, as she is my brand-new unicorn, although one with a very short fuse and temper. She is a fiery one, but she can also be mellow and compassionate. Her cause at present is the homeless. She longs to serve those in need. I also love to see her running wild towards whatever she does with her gold curls flying all over as she burns that endless energy of hers. I adore her, Mrs. V., … and we couldn't be more different! She wants to be a criminal psychologist and I don't have any idea what I want to do in life. That's how I wrote the following script to her. I wanted to memorialize our life together in its smallest details and contrast them with our polar opposites, while showing how profoundly intimate and intertwined our relations have become.

Mrs. V., it has been a great discovery for me that being so diametrically different creates some kind of 'love tension.' This in turn creates between us the sparks of endless passion, hence the name of this scribble.

"The Secret Lies in Opposite Ends at Work Forever"

You like to dance, and I don't.
You are spontaneous and blunt, and I am not.
You are loud and noisy,
I am silence personified.
You are social and friendly,
I am not very much of either.

You love certainty and predictability,

I love to improvise, never knowing what to expect.
You have a short fuse that erupts
then fades like a volcano,
my flame burns slowly for a long time.

You like to sleep late,
I rise early way before dawn.
You plan way ahead,
I do everything at the last minute.
You love to constantly organize
everything around you,
I like everything organized most of the time.

You make cleanliness and neatness
happen at all times,
I enjoy them both immensely.

You remember certain things very well,
I always remember others quite well too.

You read many people with absolute accuracy,
I always read others, but not all that well.
You love a good wine and cheese,
I am still learning to do the same.

You are a great and fast lightning cook,
I have no idea how to cook at all.

You don't care much for breakfast,

for me, it's the most important meal of the day.
You don't like ice-cream or chocolates,
I love them both to no end.

You are effusive in celebration,
I am hardly expressive on those occasions.

You play instruments with ease,
I have no clue how to do that either.

You passionately love certain kinds of music,
I love all kinds from all over the world.

You aren't physically affectionate or touchy-feely,
I am all of that, all of the time.

You can be ferociously jealous at times,
for me, those are just games people play.

You call everything by its name,
I use terms of endearment for everyone
and everything.

You like routines and predictability,
I am exactly the opposite of that.

You don't like being naked, or being barefoot,
I am quite the contrary.

You like to talk non-stop about anything,
I only do when I am passionate about something.

You like me to read to you,
I do that with gusto.

You never understand movies,
but always stay awake throughout.
I always fall asleep but somehow,
still manage to explain them to you afterward!

You always fall asleep while I drive,
I bring us both to our destination,
talking to myself the entire trip.

You hate to be behind a wheel,
I can drive forever.

You can become grumpy when bored,
those words do not exist in my vocabulary.

You never like what you order at a restaurant,
I always feed you, otherwise you help yourself
to what I've ordered.

You are cautious and fearful,
I don't understand those words either.
You are full of laughter,
Mine is hard to come by.

You love a good dress and wear it well,
I never pay any attention to my wardrobe.

We couldn't be more different about,
With whom, how, when, where,
and what we work at.
But we couldn't be more alike
in how hard we go at it!

You type super-fast,
I hardly do that at all.
Yet I read super-fast,
And you don't.

You hate to carry anything,
I love doing it for you.

You never know where you are,
I am a human compass.

You never know how to get there,
most times, I don't even need a map.

You don't know how to strike a bargain,
or negotiate a price,
I love to do both.

You believe many things are impossible,
I believe almost anything is possible,
and you've trusted me with that.

You like to sit down,

be waited on and enjoy a good meal.
I prefer self-service.

You like a good and loud fight,
I am Mr. Quiet, anti-noise and anti-fight.

You don't overlook anything you dislike,
I consciously distort reality.

You stumble and fumble all the time,
I'm not much better at that at all.

You love to browse but hardly shop,
I can't wait to get out.

You are hard to please
when you want something.
I am always dead-on, with size, type and style
when I do it for you.

Your fears disappear with board games,
where you cheat all the time.
While I am naive, clumsy, and foolish
and your easy prey each time.

Your fears go out of the window

when it comes to jumping queues,
I am always hesitant and embarrassed,
but obediently follow your lead.

You are a terrible cyclist,
I am a terrific one.

You are a great swimmer,
I, mediocre,
when doing that,
would be a superlative when doing that.

You like the coast without sand on your feet,
I was raised on the beach
and love it as it is, wild and dirty.

You like perfectly tranquil glorious weather,
the tougher and rougher it is, the better for me.

I am overwhelmingly physical,
you are always successful in slowing me down.

You are claustrophobic,
I have motion sickness.
You are afraid of heights,
I prefer rooms with a view from floor to ceiling.

You don't mind sitting in the middle,
I always sit in the front, the aisle, or facing the crowd.

You love ballet and the opera,
I love a good philharmonic orchestra and library.
We both love museums, just different parts of them.

You like to sit and munch,
I can spend hours at a bookstore
or looking at historical pictures.

You curse and use loaded words,
I never do so.

It's very hard to move on or let go,
with me, it's just a flick of a switch away.
You love to run but no longer can,
for me running is a way of life.

The things we agree on are easy to spot
and write endlessly about.
But it is on the things where we are not alike,
that healthy tension abounds.
That's why the secret lies on two opposite ends
working together forever.

I've written to her like I've never done before in my life. Perhaps this is it. This is what I love to do in life. To write or teach about it. Mrs. V., before I leave you, there is something else. Ready? I want to propose. Yes! I do. I want with all my heart for Victoria to be my wife and companion forever. But I am lost in a sea of fear and doubt. The fact is, I feel that I am nobody, I have nothing in the way of material things to offer her; I am not even certain of what I want to do in the future. Help me, please. I need your wisdom and tutelage. Waiting anxiously for your reply.

Yours truly,
Erasmus

PS. Your eternally thankful now enamored, but a lost soul mentee. By the way, I call her Vicky so that I'll never confuse her with you!

Wearing an expression of deep emotion, Professor Cromwell-Smith brings his class back to the present. His face is all lit up. His eyes seem lost in time filled with memories he is obviously comfortable with.

So, it is him, realizes the girl with the golden curls. In a whirlwind of emotions, glued to her chair with a knot in her throat and her heart racing, she does not know what to do and remains paralyzed in angst.

"When true love knocks at life's door, seize the moment and let it in, as immediately after, your heart will run the show and turn on your happiness factory. Next class, I'll take you along to the memorable occasion when Mrs. V.'s much-awaited missive finally arrived," says the inspired pedagogue to an elated audience.

Just for a fleeting moment, as most students have not yet completely stepped out of the professor's time machine, it almost seems as though countless little red hearts are floating in the air above everyone's heads.

Chapter 13

True Love and the Three-Legged Stool

He has been pedaling for more than an hour. As he takes stock of his life, Professor Cromwell-Smith wanders aimlessly around the campus back roads. To do so, he left home an hour earlier than usual. He knows that he has pursued his passions as he fulfilled his dreams. Teaching is exactly what he loves to do. What his mentors were not able to teach him though, was how to find love. Nevertheless, today's session will be about that period in his life, albeit brief when he did find it. So, he is eager to share what happened with his class. Feeling ready, he sets about heading towards the school's main building and not long thereafter he enters the auditorium to a large awaiting crowd.

"How's everyone today?" he asks.

"Awesome!" the students collectively respond in unison.

"Then let's jump right into it. Shall we?"

Today it finally happened. It arrived early in the morning, but I have not opened it yet. It has been sitting in my left pocket the entire day. It feels like it's going to burn through at any moment. I anxiously pat the flattish bulk to reassure myself that it has not yet happened, or perhaps that it will evaporate or, more realistically, that somehow, I'll lose it. Nevertheless, this self-inflicted masochism lasts the entire morning and for a very long afternoon. It is only at

day's end that I finally sit down and open Mrs. V.'s long-awaited response.

"Obsequium, obsequium, obsequious." I read aloud.

Once more her usual starting remarks are magical and feel like a precious and priceless gift.

Dear Erasmus,

I write to you with a gigantic smile on my face. Oh, my dear boy, how happy you've made me and how thoughtful of you to share some of the things that you've written for Victoria. They are a breath of fresh air allowing me into a world I once lived, until my only love was lost forever at the Battle of the Bulge. I've copied a couple of wonderful writings, that'll provide you with much needed wisdom at this magnificent crossroads in your life. The first one is simply about love. Do you know what love is? Do you know how to love? Do you know how to be loved?

"What is Love?"

What a bewildering feat,
A pair of souls
smitten with one another.
The whisperings and whistlings
of a pair of infatuated hearts,
in a world of their own.

The peace and ease
of two spirits totally comfortable
with each other,
at all times,
while enjoying
the most sublime of connections,
in a place where innate beauty
lies in bunches.

A twosome
in a state of constant flux,
where everything begins
and then continues
through endless reactions
to one another's
expressions of love.

And
by wrapping themselves around
each other's fingers,
they literally surrender to one another
and seemingly
do with each other, what they please.
And then forever spoiled,
neither is ever able to accept anything less,
but exactly the same or more,

from the other half.

That is how love becomes
a perennial exercise of
placing themselves in the other's shoes,
that is why,
love is the ultimate empathy
of two hearts
possessed by one another,
always and forever.

The second one is about true love. My boy, that's the real deal. Is this what you are feeling? What about her? Do you know that most people never experience love, and of the few that do, many let it slip away? So, let me open the doors to the magical world of true love for you...

"What is True Love?"

True love is,
when your heart does not belong to you.

True love is,
when your life's glass is only full
when with your loved one.
True love is,

when you feel that you can move mountains
or split oceans for one another.

True love hears and sees no evil as it is unconditional,
no matter the deed or mischief.

True love is,
when your skin aches
without your other half's touch,
and nothing is warmer
than being in each other's arms.

True love is,
when passion is so overwhelming,
that it's just one flick of a switch away.

True love is,
when success, defeat, or failure don't matter,
when pain and joy neither.

It is to be all for each other,
it is when we give everything, and then some.

True love, is also on the greetings
that make us jump up and down inundated in joy.
And the long embraces and farewells

that leaves us unable to swallow or breathe.
True love patiently waits and hopes
without really expecting anything in return.

True love is also a benign and forgiving stare,
smiles bursting with joy and laughter,
our life's echoes of happiness.

True love is,
when your soul mate
is part of your very essence,
when each spirit is split between both of you,
and both souls have surrendered fusing into one,
while becoming travel mates
in the topsy-turvy journey of life.

True love is,
when the colors of life
shine and blossom in full,
the bells of heaven ring,
and life's orchestra plays at its best,
and everything we feel
lies at ecstasy's zenith.

True love can't be measured.
True love can't be controlled.

True love is empowering.
True love is one of life's greatest gifts.
It is precious but many times overlooked.

True love is hard to find
perhaps you never will...
instead, it will find you!

True love is a miracle
and one of the great wonders
of being alive.

Dear infatuated mentee. Always remember, true love is not driven by success, nor does it disappear in failure. When it does arrive, it stays with you forever. Finally, in this precious little book 'The Magic in Life', there is another wonderfully written script, by the same author. It's impregnated with timeless wisdom in matters of love. It is about a three-legged stool...

"The Three-Legged Stool"

What makes a great couple?

First comes friendship,
Its foundations are honesty, loyalty,
fidelity and commitment.
In them reside communication

and the sharing of everything.

It is trusting to no end.

It is giving without expecting anything in return.

It is knowing what the other thinks without words

and knowing what the other wants

with just a glance.

It is completing each other's sentences,

complementing each other's

weaknesses and differences.

It is when respect and admiration

are the drivers and the support columns.

It is where true intimacy lies,

and where the walls and boundaries of a twosome

are built like a fortress

that provides comfort, safety, privacy, and strength

to one another.

When there is true intimacy,

our other half becomes the person

who we are comfortable with,

at all times,

who we never get tired to see, talk, or share with.

It is the person that sometimes is our parent,

some others a sibling, many others a spouse or simply a friend.

It is the person that motivates us the most,

but also calls us out

and makes us stop,

to change course or make amends.
True friendship thrives on a healthy level of tension.

And true friendship is where
for better or for worse,
in sickness or in health
and for richer or for poorer lie.

<u>Second comes Passion,</u>
When the flesh explodes without control,
when blood and desire are like a fireball,
and two bodies are insatiable
and cannot get enough of each other,
no matter how, no matter when, no matter where.
It is when lust overwhelms mind and body.
It is when one look, one touch,
one movement, one thought, one image,
is all it takes for mutual arousal to be unleashed!
It is when fantasy and imagination become reality
in a flash of flesh.
It is when everything about the other
is sensual, carnal, and seductive,
all the time and at any time.

<u>Third comes Love,</u>
True Love is when your heart
does not belong to you.

True Love is when the bells of heaven are ringing
and the trumpets of life
play heart-shaped musical notes at full throttle.
It is the delicate rose garden
that requires constant, tender care,
but produces immense,
but delicate, fragile beauty.
True Love is when your skin aches
missing the other's touch.
It is to be endlessly in awe, hopelessly infatuated,
and carelessly wrapped
around each other's fingers.
It is when nothing is warmer
than being in each other's arms.
True Love is gallantry and courtship,
it is poetry and total surrender.
It is when the colors of life
shine and blossom in full
and life's orchestra plays its best,
and everything we feel is as if
we were at ecstasy's pinnacle.
Friendship, Passion, and Love
are the three legs of a stool
that depicts a wholesome couple,
a couple that will last and endure life,
a couple that will stay together forever.

As you can see, there are three very different dimensions to a couple. Each one requires hard work. Each is distinctively different, but equally important, as all are the foundations of a continuously happy, solid and, therefore, lasting union.

Dear Erasmus, true love, once it finds you, don't ever let it go, as it may never come back or happen again for you. And, if indeed it does find you, always remember those three legs of the stool, all need to be present for your relationship to last, while still being happy. So, there you have it, is it love? Is it true love? Do you have and feel the friendship, passion, and love that constitute a lasting pair? Be happy, my son, I wish you all the best.

Your ecstatic old mentor,
Mrs. V.

PS. Erasmus, what were those little gestures that won her heart? Please tell me more about yourself, and about Vicky. Who is this enchantress that stole my beloved mentee's heart?

Professor Cromwell-Smith is overcome by emotion, and so is the student body surrounding him. For many of them, the lingering question is how and why his own three-legged stool broke. A couple of teardrops slowly make their way down the professor's pained face as his tight lips tremble slightly in a twisted bundle. A couple of students raise their hands. One is a tall freckled young man built like a linebacker, and the other is the young lady with long golden hair.

The poems, the three mentors, Oxford and Harvard! How could she have missed it? Now, there aren't any doubts. The name Victoria Emerson-Lloyd is the validation.

I must talk to him, she thinks to herself anxiously.

"Not today guys. Next time please pull me aside. Have a nice day you all," says Professor Cromwell-Smith, packing up.

At first, she feels dejected by his dismissive reply, but as the young woman with the curly blond hair sees the pained expression on the professor's face, she leaves in a hurry.

It's going to be too painful, she reflects, realizing that she won't be able to attend his next class.

After such a long time, it actually feels good, to let it all out, Professor Cromwell-Smith realizes, as he parts ways with the teary smile of someone with a broken heart.

Chapter 14

Facing a Loss

Professor Cromwell-Smith knows what it is he has tried so hard to avoid. It is not the beginning of his love story, nor the magical fairy tale that ensued along the way, but its stunning and devastating end. Today forty or some years later, today he must face the raw pain of his loss once more, but somehow the catharsis of the previous session has brought him to the right place, as today he feels calm and at peace with his feelings and beautiful parts of his past that he so dearly treasures.

Totally immersed in his thoughts, he hardly notices his arrival and parking his old bike. In the same state of absent-mindedness, he slowly paces the college halls. It is only then when he walks into the classroom that he snaps back to reality and calmly tells himself, *I am ready.* He then begins to recount the most painful period of his life...

"Hi everyone. In life, we all must deal with losses. Some are harder than others. Today, I'll share mine with you, through the prism of poetry."

Dear Mrs. V.,

I write to you with a heavy heart and the sad news that Victoria and I are no longer together. One day, she simply disappeared from campus. No note, no goodbye, her studies abandoned, her home phone disconnected. A train ride to southern Illinois was in vain. The trip merely yielded a vacated house and neighbors as surprised as me. She is gone, Mrs. V., just like that. Puff! She vanished. It's now been three months and I'll be graduating soon. I am totally lost. It is as if part of me has been yanked away. Mrs. V., it hurts deep, deep inside, but I've not given up on myself yet! Enclosed is a little something I wrote just for you...

"Sorting out the Rest"

Of all the 'ifs' and 'buts' we face,
none is more powerful
than the ones coming from those
who provide us
with life lessons,
and living tutelage.

We may pretend
we don't listen to them,
when in fact may
we hear it all.

But somewhere along the way,

hopefully sooner,

more often than later,

those words of wisdom,

almost always,

finally register.

And as we sort everything else out,

it is what was once wisely said,

what may come to us at the right time,

hopefully guiding, maybe even preventing,

or even after the fact,

helping us know what to do,

perhaps even how to mend,

for the next time around.

Mrs. V., though I've learned not to dwell on the past, rather treasure it, thus I wrote the following to evoke Victoria's presence, turning the longing and the void of her absence into a world of truly wonderful memories.

Here is something I've just written for her…

"If I Could Find You Out There"

If I could touch the stars
with my heart,
the night darkness would turn into
reds of roses and reds of fire.

If I could reach the sky
with my dreams,
the colors and tones of daylight
would turn into
inspired whites and passionate blues.

If I could morph into words,
those life moments that touch the soul
would turn into
endless shades of wisdom.

If I could simply be art,
the kind that brings
joy to the spirit,
it would turn into
greens of plenitude and yellows of life.

If I could fly to the moon
and gaze back
at Planet Earth,
it would glow like a rainbow

turning into
every color there could ever be.

But if I could only find you,
somewhere...
out there in the universe,
my dreams and my passion,
my spirit and my soul,
my life and my heart,
and all of my world,
would all,
turn into you.

If I could only find you out there,
somewhere in the Universe.

I also wrote about how I visualize her in the future. She plans to become a doctor of the mind and help criminals, and you know what? I believe she'll be masterful at it. So, I wrote to the future her, and it has helped me a great deal...

"A Labor of Love"

What a tough job
to navigate through
the darkest corners of the minds of others,
rather than your own.
Those paths where the ground is shaky

where the foundations have cracks,
where the earth moves and,
where some of the tracks of life
are blurry, without enough light,
and there is no sense of wellbeing or happiness.

But perhaps there is no tougher job
than that of dealing with minds
that not only lack meaning and purpose in life,
but are also, perhaps,
wicked, devious, reckless, or delusional,
or simply love themselves so much
that there is no room to care for anyone else.

Hence, it is only because of this
labor of deeply rooted vocational love
for the well-being of others
that such a worthy endeavor makes that big
a difference and impact on the lives of many,
the type of non-stop steady effort that addresses
every obstacle and every crisis
with resolve and genial creativity,
the kind that connects with each individual
and makes them feel and believe they are
unique, respected, and worthy,
but above all,
able to grow, overcome and have a future,

if they are willing to shape-up, do the work,
and perform at high standards.

What a tough job doing good
by improving the mindset of others in need.
What an impossible job to perform
for those in need of redemption,
those in need of a second act in life,
those that very few support or believe in.
What a tough job.
What an impossible job.
What a wonderful labor of love,
that's what you'll do,
that's what you will be leaving in your wake.
__That's what you would have done!__

What else can I do? Please share your wisdom showing me a way out of this pain.

Your amateur and aspiring poet mentee,
Erasmus Cromwell-Smith

Although somber and mystical in appearance, Professor Cromwell-Smith feels at ease, as he has just navigated, unscathed, through the most painful yet wonderful period of his life.

"Class, next time we will go over Mrs. V.'s last reply during this period, you don't want to miss it."

Today, the professor spends a good hour answering questions from a large group of students. He looks around and the young lookalike linebacker reads his mind.

"She did not come today," he informs the professor.

"Ah, all right," Professor Cromwell-Smith replies quietly.

Then he walks away to his office with an eerie feeling right in his gut.

Chapter 15

Overcoming a Loss

This morning Professor Cromwell-Smith feels blissful. After so many years, he has let in all the good memories of his one experience of true love. Leaving home, he whistles and mounts his bike with gusto.

"Truth be told, I've never found anyone else," he mumbles, as if justifying it to himself. "Excuses, excuses, and more excuses. Look at you! No family, living as if frozen in time, in a glass house behind a walled garden that's shielding you away from the world!"

Inadvertently, he snaps back at himself as his bike sways to the sides.

No, no, no, he thinks to himself. *Digging up the past unearthed all these beautiful memories. It's simple; she was and still is the love of my life.*

He argues back and forth in his mind, shedding a few tears of sheer happiness.

He quibbles, *You are far from perfect, Erasmus.* His darker side doubles down on its efforts to bring back self-inflicted wounds of the past, rattling and shaking his sunny disposition.

Self-defeating wounds won't work on me today. I feel calm and filled with wonderful memories about the true love of my life, he calmly reasons while he pedals away. Shortly thereafter, he walks into the large auditorium and faces a packed room. People are even sitting in the aisles.

This time I'll wait until the class ends. He'll surely be available, the young woman with the golden curls thinks to herself.

"Good day, class. Let us continue with the journey," says the professor.

I must confess that there are very few people I've met, that match Mrs. V.'s positive outlook and inspired attitude in life. She simply believes that every day we are alive is precious and should not be wasted, regardless of the circumstances.

Today, I am taking one of my last exams before graduation, so her letter couldn't have come at a more opportune time. It is a morale booster from my perennial and inveterate cheerleader. With much trepidation, I set aside a full hour to read the anticipated missive. Little do I know that it would turn out to be one of the best life lessons I've ever learned.

Dear Erasmus,

My heart sank when I read your letter. How very difficult it can be to lock in true love. First, love has to find you, then life circumstances and timing have to be right, but then there is us and others standing in the way, and finally, there is life itself with all its twists and turns, ups and downs.

I believe, my broken-hearted boy, that very few appreciate just how elusive, how fragile, and how ephemeral true love can be. But life goes on. Even as you long for and treasure what you had, you start piling up regrets that swallow the precious and scarce time you have left on Planet Earth. You must stay awake, my pained young soul, there are still the wonders of life to be enjoyed out there! Here is something to that effect that hopefully will catch you before regret seeps in…

"There is a Life to be Lived Out There"

Is there anything, anything
that we seek
but never reach?

Is there someone, yes, that someone
that we wait for,
but never find?

Is there anyone, anyone
that we don't need,
but never leaves?

Is there a place, that place
that we miss, but never visit?
Is there a moment
that we want back,
but is gone forever?

Is there something, yes something,
that we need,
but never seek?

Are there many, many things
that we must learn,
but never do?

Are there a few words, those words
that we could or should have said,
but never did?

Is there such a person
that brings us joy and happiness,
but we don't appreciate it?

Is there a moment in time
that we regret,
but it's too late?

Is there a friend or loved one
that gives us so much,
without asking anything in return,
but we don't value enough?
Is there a time, a moment, a place
in which we must stop or pause,
but we don't?

Is there a secret, that secret
that we must have known or shared,
but never did?

Is there a past, that past
that eventually will catch up with us,
but we never made amends to prevent it?

Is there a wait, a long wait,
that we endured to no avail,
and quit when it reoccurred?

Are there family and friends, dear family and friends
to be loved and cherished,
but we fall short?

Is there that little something,
that we should have given,
but we didn't?

Is there that true love, yes that love,
waiting for us,
but we never go for it?
Is there a God
to fear, believe, and get close to,
but we fail to do so?

Is there happiness
to be found and enjoyed everywhere,
but we don't find it?

Is there inspiration
in many little, simple,
essential things
and yet we aren't able to notice them?

Is there compassion,
to gracefully give others,
but we can't feel it ourselves?

Is there forgiveness,
to be dispensed,
but we don't act upon it?

Is there hope,
for a better life and circumstance,
but we abandon it?

Is there so much,
to be provided,
but we fail to do so?
Is there a lot needed by others,
needed by others,
but we fail to recognize it?

Is there a future not to be postponed?
Is there a world, our world,
to be seized, to be squeezed, to be lived,
with spirit and desire?

Is there a life,
without ifs or buts
without negative, regretful, or lingering grudges?

A world to give, receive and enjoy
a life, our life,
the only one we've got,
the only one we will ever have.

Yes! There is.
There is a life and a world,
ready to be lived,
waiting for all of us,
and it's happening right now.

Get out there and live. Don't cut yourself any slack, as being in love with someone that is no longer there does not prevent you from living in full. Young Erasmus, life is not to be lived from the sidelines. Bottom line, we all want to be happy, but it is on all of us to crack the riddle of joyousness. Rest assured that the key to solving it is to never detach but rather be absolutely immersed in your life. My dear, the following writing is something I treasure very much and always keep handy and often go back to, and I hope you will as well…

"Life's True Success is Being Happy"

Life is not a spectator's sport,
if you want to be entertained, you will,
as life will offer you countless options
to choose from a never-ending carousel.

But once the show is over,
the fun and the thrill of it all will escape in a hurry,
as being a spectator makes it impossible
to capture and retain
the passion and the purpose of what others did.

Feeling good for long never happens
to the bystander,
as the emptiness of a life without meaning
will sink in when you are alone
at night with your own pillow.

You can celebrate and rejoice for
the victories and defeats of others all you want,

but it'll only last a fleeting moment,
because in the end, you are still you
and nothing has changed.

Life, to the contrary, is a participant's sport
where you play with passion and purpose
and in turn bring happiness and meaning,
and they last only as long as
you continue to churn and churn
pouring your heart into everything that you do.

A life with passion and purpose
is one in which you are its main participant.
It's a life where you rise and fall, you win and lose,
you love and are loved back in return,
where you give a lot more
than you receive or take in.
It's a life where you dare, stumble and endure,
and never stop trying or give up!

It is a life
in which you are endlessly curious
and always learning.

It is a life
in which you are totally immersed.

It's a life with meaning, it's life at its fullest!

It is one where happiness is not pursued but ensues
as a result of deliberate involvement
in a wholesome living experience.

Because in the end what you really want is success,
what you are really after is achievement.

But there is no success or achievement
of any kind as a spectator,
only fun and intensity
that are both shallow and passing.

Success does not belong
to spectators or bystanders.
They belong to life's players, those that are involved,
'The Participants'

life's true and highest level of success,
is being happy,
one where you can never cease
to be totally engaged in,
whereby you create a virtuous circle
that never ends.

Young Erasmus, life's clock is ticking. Your life's battery is wasting away. Believe me, you don't want to wake up one morning and realize that your life is over. But let me caution you, after a breakup one must be especially wary of falling in love right afterward, in particular when only driven by wealth and success. It can easily fool your heart. Passions of such a kind are not genuine, but just mere infatuations, impregnated with the emptiness of material things. Instead of the comforting security they are supposed to provide, they only offer you sadness and solitude, especially when you are all alone at night with your own pillow. I don't know if there is enough time left at Harvard, but if so, do me a favor and this time do it for me:

FIND YOURSELF A SWEET, DEVOTED AND LOVING GIRLFRIEND.

Dear boy, one last matter of importance. I know we will be seeing you back home soon after your graduation. I say this because Mr. Morris, Mr. Newton, and yours truly have prepared for you alone a special joint meeting, and by unanimous consent have named it 'The Final Session.' It'll bring to an end to your formal tutelage from this eclectic trio.

Take great care of yourself. Especially now when you are so vulnerable. Farewell, my boy.

Love you dearly,
Mrs. V.

The young woman with the curly blond hair cries in silence, then she quietly slips away, not able to finish the class.

I understand so much more now, she reasons to herself as she realizes that she'll miss him again.

Professor Cromwell-Smith stares at his class with humble gratitude as everyone comes back to the present.

"Next class will be our final session as was back then for me as well," he says, smiling as he scouts the crowd. The young lady is no longer in the room.

She was there earlier. Well, hopefully next session I'll catch up with her, he thinks.

Then as they all walk out, a group of students surrounds the professor.

"You look a lot better, sir," one of them comments.

"Indeed, I do, certainly an unexpected bend in the road. Just a short while ago I was close to death. I had few weeks to live, but now I am healthy again. That's life, you see. How else would I've been able to share my story with you?"

The professor walks on, and students are left with a collective feeling of nostalgia. They are all eager to experience Cromwell-Smith's final session, but at the same time wish his class would never end.

Chapter 16

The Happiness Formula

Erasmus Cromwell-Smith is sweating profusely as he works his way cycling the campus streets. The early summer morning heat hit him the moment he opened his door. Even as he breathes, he feels certain heat in his throat. Other than his perspiration, he is ready.

Arriving at the faculty building, he walks briskly while mopping his face with his wrinkled handkerchief.

"Good morning you all," he says to a crowd even larger than that of his previous class.

"All right let's do it," the professor says as he sighs, breathing in deeply.

"Throughout the past few months, you've joined me on a journey of discovery and wisdom. Poetry has been our telescope through which we gaze at the wonderful universe of life. Today we bring it all to a close with what proved to be one of the most memorable moments of my life."

Having graduated from Harvard I visit home one last time before permanently relocating to America. Upon my arrival, I am ceremoniously summoned by my three mentors through a beautiful hand-painted invitation to a grand final session. After sharing more wisdom and art, they will formally end their tutelage.

Two days after my arrival, at the agreed hour, I walk into Mr. M.'s store and find my three mentors there, relaxed and smiling, gazing at my entrance with benign eyes. They effusively pile on me, including bear hugging and all. For a moment, it seems that I have three additional parents for a total of five.

Mr. M. then pulls out a large, folded page and affixes it to a blackboard in front of me. I see a triangle drawn on the sheet.

"Dear mentee, we present to you... The Happiness Formula. It is a fitting conclusion to our mentorship. Along with the many other lessons you've received, I am certain it will help you live an inspired and blissful life," he announces.

My three mentors stare at me. They have all returned to their usual behavior. Strict and stern. Articulate and yet demanding. Then I start to review the geometrical figure.

Professor Cromwell-Smith briefly interrupts the magical journey into the past to turn on his tablet and the auditorium's projector. In seconds the image of a triangle is illuminated on the screen for all to see. He then continues to narrate…

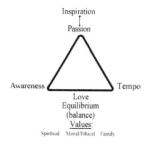

As I contemplate the figure in wonder, Mr. M. walks over and places his hands over my shoulder.

"My eternally curious mentee, what this figure shows you is that there are three simultaneous attitudes to pursue in life for happiness to ensue. First, find your passions and live them in full. Second, maintain a tempo, adequate for your passions, and thirdly, be continuously aware and involved with your life, capturing every moment, and always be grateful for whatever you've got. Sitting below are three essential building blocks that are the Happiness Triangle's foundations.

"The first is love, the key to unlock your heart's treasures, powers, and strengths. The second is equilibrium (balance), which is only possible through a stable emotional life acting as the support wire. Third, at the base, are our family, moral, and spiritual values. This is the root of all the foundations that support the Happiness Triangle. Finally, these three attitudes and support blocks are equally important, as they are all genuine sources of happiness. They are all tightly connected to and interdependent of one another. This happiness ecosystem is where inspiration is born and where it thrives, propelling us to a noble condition of sublime desire and a highly functional state that brings out the best in all of us. Always remember this Erasmus, an inspired person is a wizard, a life wizard!" teaches Mr. M. gleefully.

"Young apprentice, the three of us have collaborated long and hard to create this final gift. It encompasses what we have taught you.

Both the triangle and this scribble describe a life path that we all wish you to pursue in life," Mr. N. says.

He then asks me to read the scribble. As I start, I realize that it contains the happiness formula in detail.

"The Happiness Formula"

Sometimes <u>we hope,</u> that simply by being alive,
happiness would be something we will find
or stumble upon with utmost certainty.
But waiting for happiness to occur
by chance or luck
is the equivalent of a reward
without merits or a prize
without struggle or effort.

In other moments <u>we wish,</u>
that happiness would be cast through a magic spell,
an incantation a dream or an illusion.
But there aren't too many sorcerers among us,
as 'life wizards' are very hard to find,
since the formula to morph dreams into happiness
is an exceptional virtue that very few possess.

Why is happiness so elusive,
unexpected, and ephemeral?
Can we ever find it, and if we do, would we know it?

If so, would we enjoy it?
Would we be appreciative of the privilege
and treasure it afterwards forever?

Some believe that
in order to obtain happiness,
it must be pursued.
Hence, it is a derivation
from a deliberate chase
or pursuit to make it happen.

There are others who, to the contrary,
believe that happiness ensues,
as a 'consequence of' or is 'subsequent to,'
and therefore,
it is the outcome of the pertinent ways
we choose to live our lives.

Then there are those who believe that happiness
only occurs in the face of tragedy and sorrow.
But tragic optimism, pain, and suffering
are rarely a path to ecstasy!

So, how do we find happiness?
Do we find it
through the intention and the desire to be happy?

Or do we find it
through the paths and roads
we wilfully take towards the land of joy,
or through both?

The answer lies in the Happiness Formula, which has
three interconnected life attitudes and three supporting blocks.

First,
find your Passion.
Passion is your life's engine.
Find what you love and do it,
recognize what you are passionate about
and stick to it, for it will greatly enhance the chances
that your strongest talents and abilities
will be put to good use,
and that you'll be performing,
in whatever your endeavor is,
to the best of your abilities.

To do what you love is easy
and the amounts of effort, energy, determination,
discipline, and persistence required
become unimportant, without obstacles.

When you do what you love,

it brings you the greatest amount of
satisfaction, pride, and sense of accomplishment.

When you do what you are passionate about,
you'll never find ifs, buts, or excuses to get started,
nor would you talk yourself into inaction
or avoid your duties and responsibilities,
but to be a master at anything
takes time, growth, maturity, determination,
failure, innate talent, and passion!

Second,
productivity requires tempo.
Tempo is the RPM of your life engine.
It is the pace at which you execute the delivery.
It is about how efficient you are.
Without rhythm and tempo,
you're quickly overwhelmed
and your life's engine slows down.
In today's world an engine without the right RPM,
overheats and overloads in a heartbeat.
To multitask
and cope with the pace of modern life,
to be highly functional
and to be able to sustain a high tempo,
you'll need to constantly re-train yourself

so you can perform at a tempo
commensurate with your goals.

And third,
being alive requires awareness.
<u>*Capture your life through awareness.*</u>
We cannot be bystanders in our own lives,
we must be totally involved,
we must be active participants,
capturing each moment
exactly as it is dealt to us.
We can't postpone our lives.
We can't afford to let our precious time
on planet earth,
be just about day after day rolling
on top of each other
whilst we watch in a catatonic, zombie-like state.
We must be eternally grateful
for what we have and receive every day
and well as for our travel companions in life.

Passivity is out of the question,
action is an existential imperative!

Finally, life gives us minute signs,
tiny but crucially important messages

that contain clues
that without awareness we may not be able to see,
as if we were walking blindly through it.

One thing is absolutely certain:
these light bulbs will be scattered
along our journey's path,
sometimes as symbols of life,
sometimes as calls to action
or simply as warning signs,
but all of them waiting for us
to be spotted and figured out as if they were puzzles
that once solved, will light up our way,
enabling us to move forward in life,
with a fully lit road ahead of us.

But three supporting blocks are needed for happiness to thrive.

First,
you need love to be happy.
<u>Love is the foundation of happiness.</u>
True love is when
your heart does not belong to you.
Focus on giving out of your heart
and do it with passion.

Second,

you need a balance between fun and work.

Set and keep your priorities in balance.

Balance only exists through

a solid emotional life underneath.

Equilibrium is born out of practice

and a healthy lifestyle.

And third,

happiness thrives on solid values.

Character and virtue are built from

spiritual, moral, and family values

through faith, truth, honesty

and unbreakable bonds of love.

Out of his happiness ecosystem of three attitudes,

(passion, tempo, and awareness)

and the three foundations supporting them,

(love, balance, and values)

is where inspiration is born,

where inspiration thrives,

and propels us into

a noble condition of sublime desire

and a highly functional state

that brings out the best in all of us,

generating continuous happiness.

Inspiration may well be
the only source of continuous happiness.
<u>*Inspiration is the stuff of wizards,*</u>
<u>*life wizards!*</u>

As I finish, Mr. M. continues.

"Erasmus, here is a summary of the happiness formula," he says in a business-like tone, as if trying to separate himself from his emotions. Then he starts to read...

Love, Equilibrium (Balance) and Values
are the foundations of
Awareness, Passion, and Tempo.

When we truly love,
when we have a balanced lifestyle,
when we live according to our family, moral/ethical and spiritual
values,
we have the keys to continuous happiness.

Then,

When we do what we love and do it with passion,
when we live with intensity, rhythm, and tempo,
when we capture, squeeze,
and 'live' every moment we are alive,

and when we focus on giving
and do it as well with passion,

WE ARE SIMPLY HAPPY!

Each of them is
a true and legitimate source of happiness.

But the ultimate source of constant happiness
is a noble state of sublime desire,
a heightened level of hypersensitivity,
that brings the best out of all of us
and this is,

INSPIRATION!

This leads us to be inspired,
to be Inspired Persons, life wizards,
and to live

AN INSPIRED LIFE!

And that's it! My tutelage has ended. My three mentors gather around me and in total silence, each shakes my hand firmly, albeit rather briefly. Aside from a very effusive kiss on the cheek by Mrs. V., this is otherwise a rather solemn moment. As I leave my

melancholic mentors, I feel an immense sense of pride and gratitude
towards each one of them.

"I am ready for life. World, here I go...!" I say, my parting words
to the waving trio standing at the doorstep of Mr. M.'s shop, as I
walk upon the cobblestones on my way home.

Professor Cromwell-Smith is elated but emotionally spent, as if he has just crossed the finish line of a long race where all the competitors wore different shades of himself. He knows he is done as he has run out of words.

"Thank you all. This was..."

He then gestures with both hands like an orchestra conductor, and the audience reads him, so everyone joins him, and they all proclaim in unison...

"INSANELY AWESOME!"

With a big broad smile, he bows his head in respect and he has nothing else to add, but life does.

As the echo dies, the entire auditorium stands up to applaud and cheer. That is when he sees her in the crowd, the young, curly blond-haired girl raising her hand, jumping up and down, trying to draw his attention.

Interrupting the crowd, the professor yells, "One moment please!"

"How can I help you, young lady?" he asks.

Abruptly, then like there is no tomorrow, she begins to talk.

181

"Professor Cromwell-Smith, I first came to one of your classes last year as you were reading a wonderful Pablo Neruda poem. I promised myself at that moment, that I was going to attend your entire course this year. It turned out to be one of the most transcendental decisions I've taken in my life. I didn't know then, none of us knew, that you were going to veer off-curriculum and share your life with us through poetry. From the very first class, a picture began to emerge. Way before you fell in love within your life story, I knew," she says.

"Professor, my mom has never stopped loving you. That's why I did not have the fortitude to come to one of your last classes, as I assumed correctly that it was going to be about the breakup. Mother's parents simply did not want her to marry you, but rather someone they had chosen since her childhood. That's how she came to marry my father and had three children, of whom I am the youngest. When my father died last summer, after five years of agonizing illness, we all three decided to find the man she so adores, reveres, and worships: you. God works in mysterious ways, Professor. It did not take us long to find you and in my case to get to know you and understand, first-hand, my mother's other half. Her only true love in life."

The knot in Professor Cromwell-Smith's throat renders him unable to speak or breathe for a moment. Then, when he gathers the strength to speak, another unexpected bend in the road awaits him.

A voice from the past comes at him from the very top of the stands.

"Erasmus!" a voice exclaims.

182

Looking up, he sees her for the first time after forty-some years. The familiar voice and tone has a touch of hesitation, perhaps anguish. It is deeply emotional, even primal. It is at the same time a lament and a plea, both on the verge of succumbing to pure joy-saturated love, as it comes straight from the longing heart of his other half.

"I am right here," she proclaims.

"I am right here, my love," she affirms, as time comes to a standstill and true love graces them both once more.

Parting words by the author,

My parents' love story went on for another twenty-five years. Life was going to provide them yet with another unexpected bend in the road when my grandmother's eldest daughter, Elizabeth Victoria, and her husband Jordan, my biological parents, were killed in a road accident. As a consequence, Erasmus and Victoria, who at the time was my grandmother, adopted and raised me as their son and that's why I consider them my parents. And so it was, theirs was a 'true love' story and they indeed lived happily ever after. And this is the second existential reason why I decided to tell this story, as by doing so, their lives would be honored and preserved. In the end, one glaring question still lingers unanswered. Why did my father never reply to Mrs. V.'s request about how he won my mother's heart? Perhaps that, and their lives together before and after the breakup, is a rabbit hole worth pursuing.

Erasmus Cromwell-Smith II.
Written at
T.D.O.K.
March 6th, 2050.

Chronology

1954	1958	1976	1977
Erasmus born.	Victoria born.	Erasmus & Victoria meet.	Victoria vanishes

1978	1984	1995	1997
Victoria marries.	Victoria graduates as Criminal Psychologist.	Victoria's 1st. child born.	Victoria's 2nd. child born.

1999	2011	2016	2017
Victoria's 3rd child born.	Victoria's husband diagnosed with cancer	Victoria's husband dies	Erasmus & Victoria reunite.

2018	2019	2042	2050
Victoria's first grandchild Erasmus II born.	Erasmus II parents killed on road accident. Erasmus & Victoria adopt him.	Within a month of each other Victoria & Erasmus pass away.	Erasmus II writes **The Happiness Triangle**

Acknowledgement

To the ad-hoc members of *The Equilibrist* series pseudo editor's committee, you are an eclectic and diverse group of published authors, historians, pedagogues, and intellectuals. But first and foremost, you are all serious readers. Adam, Andric, Barry, Christian, Mark, Mitch, Rafael, Tony and Willy, your feedback was invaluable. As important though, was all of you having a strong emotional connection and reaction to the book. It was highly fulfilling and inspirational, making the end of a very intense journey, even more so.
Thank you.

To my team, Amy, Ana Julia (RIP), Alfredo, Andrea, Charles, Elisa, Maria Elena, and MaryAnn (RIP). Without your talent, belief, motivation and hard work, this book would not have been possible.

Finally, it is only because of my family's blind faith and support that I was able to carry out this work independently and unconstrained of any commercial editing or vetting filters, which resulted in making *The Equilibrist* series a genuine and authentic creation. You enabled me to release to the world a craft that is exacting, word by word, to the way I intended and to the form I created it. Thank you as well.

About the author:

Erasmus Cromwell-Smith II is an American writer, playwright, and poet. *The Happiness Triangle,* part of *The Equilibrist* series, was crafted through a very intense, intimate, and introspective dive into the author's own life experience and wisdom. It is his first published work.